EVER SO
HUMBLE

Other books by Fran Shaff:

The Love Trap
Montana Match

EVER SO HUMBLE

•

Fran Shaff

AVALON BOOKS
NEW YORK

PRINTED IN THE UNITED STATES OF AMERICA
ON ACID-FREE PAPER
BY HADDON CRAFTSMEN, BLOOMSBURG, PENNSYLVANIA

For JC, Jim, and Zack.

Chapter One

As the lift doors closed, an uneasiness began to fill the musty car. The tall, lean man in the brown polo shirt and khaki pants seemed to pose no physical threat, but Marisa sensed she was somehow at risk with him.

The elevator began to move. Several feet into the ride, it came to an abrupt halt.

The air seemed to thicken, or at least it was becoming more difficult to breathe. Marisa smiled nervously at her companion. "I hate it when this happens."

He reached for the emergency phone. "I'll call for help, and we'll be out in a minute."

"Don't bother," Marisa said. "The phone doesn't work. It hasn't worked for months."

The man drew his hand back. "You're sure?"

Marisa shrugged. "I'm sure it hasn't worked for months, but I guess I'm not certain if by some miracle it might have been fixed in the last few days. You might as well give it a try."

He reached for the phone and attempted to call.

"You're right," he said, returning the phone to the receiver. "It doesn't work."

Marisa took a deep breath. "I wish I were wrong. I hate being stuck in this thing."

"You've been stuck in here before?" he asked, his eyebrow rising high over one of his dark brown eyes.

Marisa swallowed hard and nodded. "A couple of times."

"How long did you have to wait to be rescued?" The man was as cool as iron.

"Thirty minutes the first time, an hour and a half the second."

He glanced at his watch. "I've got an appointment in an hour." He smiled comfortably. "I hope we're out of here by then."

Marisa stepped back and leaned against a wall, grabbing the brass handrail to steady herself. His smile had made her even shakier than the confinement. "I wouldn't mind getting out right now. I wish I'd taken the stairs." She took a deep breath. "Maybe the new owner of the building will fix this ancient elevator."

"Someone should," he said, looking around the forlorn car.

Marisa folded her arms and steeled her jaw. "A lot of good it would do to fix this old thing. Most of us probably won't be here to enjoy it."

He lifted his brow again. "Why's that?"

She pulled her sleeveless yellow shirt over her cutoffs. "Because the new owner wants to turn this building into condominiums. Many of us tenants cannot afford to buy our apartments."

He shrugged. "Maybe you could."

She narrowed her focus on him. "Who are you anyway?"

He extended his hand toward her. "I'm Lee. I moved in a couple of days ago, the fifth floor."

Marisa took Lee's hand. The moment she touched him she felt her skin tingle. "Marisa Orlando. I'm on the third floor."

"It's a pleasure to meet a new neighbor." He let go of her hand.

"Are you new to Houston?"

"I grew up here, did some moving around and returned a few years ago."

Their casual conversation and the warmth in his tone helped Marisa begin to relax. "You like it here then?"

His smile filled his entire face. "Very much."

"There's no better place to live."

The elevator lurched and Marisa jumped forward.

Lee reached toward her, almost touching her arm. "You okay?"

She lifted her eyes to meet his. "Fine," she lied. Between a jumpy elevator and a handsome man's unsettling proximity, how could she be okay?

He casually pulled his outstretched hand back. "What do you do, Miss Orlando?"

Marisa took a deep breath and leaned against the wall to steady herself. "I'm a teacher."

"Let me guess," he said, his fingers toying with a loose strand of lignitic hair on his forehead. "Third grade?"

Marisa shook her head. "Not even close. Seventh grade."

"Wow! That's not an easy age to handle."

"You're a teacher too?"

He rubbed his hand over the wheat-colored skin of his strong jaw. "No, but I remember how obnoxious I was at

that age. If your students are anything like I was, your job
isn't an easy one."

"No, it isn't, but I've done it for six years now, ever
since I graduated from college. I think I'm getting the
hang of it."

He nodded amiably, then looked around the car.
"There's a door up there," he said, pointing to the ceiling.
"I can't reach it, but if I lift you up on my shoulders
maybe you could see how near we are to the next floor."

Marisa felt her back weld to the wall. "Are you kidding? No way!"

"All you have to do is lift the lid and look up. I'll hang
on to you tightly. I won't let you fall."

It wasn't the fall she was afraid of. He'd made her nervous ever since she got into the elevator with him. Now he
wanted to put his hands on her? He'd stirred up her emotions enough just shaking her hand.

"Let's wait for help."

"You're sure you don't mind?"

Those engaging eyes of his and that provocative grin
sent charges of electricity through Marisa. "Of course, I
mind being stuck in here, but, at the moment, I don't mind
enough to climb up and take a look into an elevator shaft."

"All right," he said agreeably, "then we might as well
make the best of the situation." He reached down and
picked up a sack next to him which Marisa hadn't noticed
before. He put his hand inside and pulled out two bottles of
root beer. "Thirsty?" he asked, handing her a soft drink.

Marisa accepted his hospitality. "It's cold."

"I bought it from that little convenience store up the
street just before I got on the elevator. I've been dying for
something to drink. It's so hot."

"And this elevator is as stuffy as they come."

He twisted the cap off his soft drink and drank.

"Would you like to sit down?" He waved his arm about the car. "I'm sorry the sofa hasn't arrived yet."

Marisa chuckled at the humor he used to try to put her at ease. She seated herself on the floor and decided Lee must be a very nice man. He'd done nothing but try to make her more comfortable since the elevator stalled.

Lee sat a few feet away from her. "You have a lovely smile, Marisa."

She couldn't stop the heat that warmed her cheeks. "Thank you."

"How's your root beer?"

"Hits the spot," she said. She took a deep breath and tried to feel more at ease with the attractive stranger.

"Would you like some pretzels or donuts?"

She shook her head. "Pretzels and donuts?" she asked, raising her eyebrows. "Looks like you're missing most of the four food groups."

He chuckled lightly. "What can I say? I don't like to cook. I do love junk food."

Marisa sipped more root beer as she nodded agreeably and replied to his smile with a smidgen of a grin.

"I hope you're not going to be as late for an appointment as I will be if this car doesn't get moving soon," Lee said casually.

"I'm afraid I was running late before I stepped on the elevator."

"I'm sorry."

Marisa waved a hand nonchalantly. "It isn't your fault."

For a moment, Lee looked guilty enough for this accident to actually be his fault.

"I'm on my way to see my mother. She's in a nursing home."

"And she's waiting for your arrival."

She nodded and took another sip of her root beer.

"Is she very ill?"

"She had a stroke. Her recovery has been unbearably slow. She's still so helpless." Marisa felt her eyes moisten and her throat begin to constrict. "She'll be there for a long time, I'm afraid. It seems like she's been there forever already."

Lee glanced away then looked back at her with sympathetic eyes. "I'm sorry, Marisa."

She studied his deep brown eyes with golden flecks. "I appreciate that," she said softly. The look of concern he gave her was both warm and unsettling. The reality of their confinement gripped her hard all of a sudden. Marisa jumped to her feet and grabbed her copper-colored hair in despair. "Why doesn't this thing move?"

Lee didn't budge. "It will, Marisa," he said reassuringly. "We'll be out soon, I'm sure."

He was calming her again. He could tell she was uncomfortable, but did he know that being alone with him was more disconcerting than being stuck in the elevator? Marisa stared at the elevator door. "I hope so."

"Have you ever tried the tacos or hamburgers at Pat O'Reiley's Mexican Restaurant?"

The abrupt change of subject shifted her focus. "The restaurant two blocks from here?"

"Yeah. I heard he makes the best burgers in town."

She sat down again, but not too close to Lee, his proximity was just too unsettling. "It's sort of a hangout for the people in the neighborhood. He's got everything from burgers to enchiladas and pizzas."

"Looks like maybe I found my antidote to junk food.

I'm sure I can force down a salad once in a while with a burger, pizza or a taco or two."

Marisa couldn't help but smile at his joke. "Then I won't have to worry about your diet," she said, teasing him.

He raised his eyebrows. "You'd worry about me? But you just met me."

Her cheeks began to burn with embarrassment over his reaction to her gentle barb. "I'm concerned about all of my neighbors," she said a little too defensively. "You'll find we're a very tight-knit group in this building."

He eyed her carefully as he drank from his soda bottle. "I see."

The anxiety of confinement took hold of Marisa once more. She stood and went to the emergency phone. She lifted it and listened. She pressed a few buttons on the elevator panel, then slammed the phone back into its place. "This is ridiculous!"

Lee stood behind her. He placed his hands on her shoulders. "Easy, Marisa. You're doing just fine."

His breath fanned her neck. He stood seven or eight inches taller than her five feet, four inches, and she could sense his broad build warming the air behind her. He was trying to comfort her, but his nearness, his unsettling touch only made her heart beat faster.

"We won't have to wait much longer," he said, gently squeezing her shoulders. "I'm sure of it."

Wait longer? She couldn't wait another minute. Lee was much too close. He was touching her again, consoling her, and the intimacy was much too unnerving and too inviting. Everything within her was beginning to turn inside out.

She pulled away from Lee and spun to face him. "Still want to try lifting me up to the trap door?"

"I thought you were afraid."

She lifted a shoulder and let it fall. "I am, but I hate to keep my mother waiting." That was a plausible reason for her change of heart, Marisa decided.

He touched a finger to her chin. "You don't have to be afraid, Marisa. I'll hold on to you tightly. I won't let you fall."

She nodded thoughtfully and swallowed hard. "I trust you," she said.

"Ready?"

She nodded determinedly.

He lifted her up and placed her on one of his shoulders. "Can you reach the door?"

She stretched her arms and lifted the lid. "Yes, but I need to be a little higher to look out."

"Climb on my shoulder so you can stand." He held her with one hand and placed the other at the bottom of her foot so she could propel herself up.

His hand slid over her leg as Marisa maneuvered her body higher. In the midst of her fearful activities, as Lee's fingers glided over her skin, the only thing besides the warmth of Lee's touch that drifted through Marisa's mind was the fact that she was glad she'd shaved her legs that morning.

He held the calf of one leg and the thigh of the other as she stood on his shoulders. "See anything, Marisa?"

She peered into the dark shaft a long moment, then lowered herself.

Lee brought her back to his shoulder before he returned her to her feet next to him. "Well?"

"The door above is six feet away or more. We'll just have to wait."

He glanced up at the trap door then fixed his gaze on Marisa. "It won't be much longer."

She looked around the motionless elevator car which held them captive. "The new owner has had people over here working on the exterior of the building."

"I know."

"Maybe he'll get this elevator fixed soon."

"Maybe."

She lifted her red curls from her shoulders, folded her arms and gazed up at him. "I don't know what I'm going to do if this building does go condo as rumor has it."

"Why's that?"

Marisa tightened her grasp on her arms and lifted her chin. "I can't afford to buy my apartment. I'm lucky to be able to pay the rent."

"Maybe your payments won't be any higher than your rent."

"Yeah, right," she scoffed, "fat chance." She narrowed her focus on him. "I've heard some things about this L. C. Ramon. He's turned old apartment buildings into posh units for the rich all over the country. He makes millions of dollars off his apartment buildings."

"Does he?" Lee asked, raising his eyebrow.

"Yes. He's renovated buildings here in Houston, in Chicago and in Dallas, too. He's made a fortune, several fortunes."

"Really?" A twinkle appeared in Lee's eye as though he admired the man.

"Yes, really. Now he's got his hands on our building. You and I and all the rest of the tenants will soon be out on the street."

"Have you been given an eviction notice?"

"Not yet."

"Have you talked to the other tenants about this?"

"Not yet."

"Maybe you should. Maybe the other tenants would like the idea of owning their own homes."

Marisa unfolded her arms brusquely. "Of course, they'd like to own their homes. Everyone likes to own a home. I used to own one, but I had to give it up. Mom's medical expenses were too high. The apartment I have in this building is the best I could find for the money. I'll never find another apartment as nice as the one I have for the same rent. Besides, the people who live here are more than neighbors to me. They're my friends."

He bit his lip and draped his arms across his chest.

"Most of the other tenants earn little more than minimum wage, or they're retired, disabled or out of work." She lifted her chin. "Are you working, Lee?"

"Yes. I'm in construction."

She nodded thoughtfully. "Then maybe you could afford to buy your apartment. Construction work pays better than minimum wage."

"I think I could manage it."

"And you've just moved in. You're lucky. What about the people who've been living here for years? This is their home. Now they'll have to leave."

"Marisa," he said, stuffing his hands into the pockets of his khaki pants, "if you're afraid of the new owner's plans or upset about them, why don't you do something about it?"

"Like what?"

"Set up an appointment with him and see if he'll talk business. Find out what his intentions are for the building. He can't be all bad. As you said, he's already making repairs to the exterior of the building. I noticed that there had been a problem with a leak in my apartment, but there was no sign of any water coming in during that downpour we had last night."

"I suppose I could talk to him. It's possible he'd be a reasonable man."

"Anything's possible."

Marisa thought a minute and glanced around the elevator. Then she shook her head. "I'd probably be wasting my time. He's going to turn this building into a palace for the rich like he did the other buildings."

Lee gave her a questioning look. "How do you know that? Where did you get all your information about Ramon?"

"I do read a newspaper once in a while."

The corner of his mouth lifted slightly. "Maybe you shouldn't believe everything you read."

The elevator lurched.

Marisa and Lee struggled to maintain their balance.

"I hope that movement means this relic is ready to start doing its job again," Marisa said.

Lee leaned his shoulder against the wall of the elevator. "This hasn't been so bad," he said, reaching to tuck a lock of fiery hair behind Marisa's shoulder. He pulled his hand back. "I've enjoyed getting to know you."

Marisa could feel her cheeks matching the color of her hair. "I can think of better places to get to know someone."

"Me, too," Lee said softly. "Like Pat O'Reiley's Mexican Restaurant."

Marisa smiled.

"You could join me there for dinner some time. We could get to know each other a little better."

"I could," she said coyly, surprising herself with the ease in her response.

The elevator started moving upwards.

Lee glanced up, then back at Marisa. "It looks like we're moving in the right direction."

Marisa was relieved by the elevator's movement. She grinned at Lee's subtle implication and tilted her head. "I was on my way out, not up."

"Wherever you were going when you got on the elevator, we're both going the same way now."

She smiled broadly at the double meaning in his words. She liked Lee. She was more than just attracted to him. She genuinely liked him.

"Which apartment are you in on the third floor? I'll stop by later and set a time for that dinner at Pat O'Reiley's."

"3-C."

Lee nodded toward her. "I look forward to seeing you again."

The elevator door opened.

Lee stepped into the hall of the fifth floor.

"Lee," Marisa called, holding the lift door open, "you didn't tell me your last name."

He stared back at her for a moment, then said, "It's Ramon. I'm Lee Charles Ramon."

The hand Marisa was using to hold the elevator door open flew to her throat. The doors closed, prohibiting her from making the exit to the stairway she had intended to take to the first floor.

Marisa felt her eyes grow, her throat tighten and her belly flip-flop. The lift descended, taking her back to the ground floor. The man she let get under her skin during her brief confinement in the musty elevator was the new owner of the building, L. C. Ramon.

Chapter Two

To say she was distracted during her visit with her mother would be a gross understatement. Marisa could think of little else besides Lee Charles Ramon as she helped her mother with her nails and her hair. She'd felt as though she'd been betrayed by a close friend when she learned the delightful man she'd met in the elevator was her nemesis. No matter how kind Lee had been during their confinement in the elevator, he wasn't her friend. He was a stranger, a man who would be making changes to the building, changes that could affect her shrinking wallet, changes that may cause her to have to leave the home and friends she'd grown to love.

Marisa gazed at her mother. She was so helpless and unresponsive. How Marisa wished she could talk to her mom the way she used to. She missed their conversations so much. She couldn't help but wonder if the iron-willed Ariane Orlando would ever be able to walk or talk or communicate again.

It seemed as though Marisa's life continued to get

worse. First her mother's stroke, followed by the after-
math of the unbearable disability, then the unending bills
that took away the house and car Marisa owned and continued to eat at most of her salary. She barely had enough
money to pay the rent on her apartment and keep herself
fed. If her housing costs went up by a mere fifty dollars a
month, she'd be looking for another apartment.

She wanted to cry at the prospect of moving again, but
she was not going to cry. She had to stop feeling sorry for
herself. She had to find L. C. Ramon and discover exactly
what he was going to do with the building. Were she and
her neighbors going to be evicted or not? One way or the
other, she had to know what life held for her.

When she returned home, Marisa devoured a baloney
sandwich. Then she prepared to face Lee.

A knock sounded at her door just as she was about to
leave. Marisa opened the door.

A panic-stricken Randi Jarvis stood in the hall holding
the hand of her seven-year-old son Cliff. "Marisa, I'm
desperate. My baby-sitter backed out on me. Can you
watch Cliff? I won't be gone long. My boss called, and he
needs help serving a banquet. I'll get a hundred dollars
for only two hours work."

Marisa opened her door wide. "You can't pass that up,
Randi. I'll be happy to watch Cliff for you."

Randi placed a hand over her heart. "You're a lifesaver,
Marisa."

"No problem, Randi. I'm glad to help. Cliff and I are
good friends," she said, smiling at the blond-haired boy.

"Can I play your piano?" He always asked to play her
piano.

Marisa stuck her fingers in the boy's lemony curls and
rubbed his head. "It's still out of tune, sport, but I happen

to have some construction paper and markers. Maybe you could make your mom a work of art for her refrigerator."

Cliff gave an exaggerated nod. "Okay," he said as though the word were actually two words.

Randi glanced at her watch, then back at Marisa. "I'll be back in about three hours." She pulled a slip of paper from her pocket. "Here's the number where I can be reached if you need to call me."

Marisa took the paper and put it in the pocket of her cutoffs. "Don't worry about a thing. I have some reading to do, and Cliff can work on his art."

Randi opened the door and stepped into the hall. "Thanks, Marisa."

Marisa watched Randi head for the stairway, then she closed the door. It always amazed her how much Cliff and Randi looked alike. Both of them had exactly the same shade of blond hair and blue eyes. Their skin was very fair, and, since Mac had died, Randi was as thin as her little boy too. Randi seemed to have lost her appetite both for food and for life when she lost her husband. The young mother did the best she could, but it sure wasn't easy. Anyone could see that.

Marisa went to the desk where she kept her school supplies and dug out scissors, construction paper and markers. She set Cliff up at the table in her kitchen. Within minutes the boy was engrossed in creativity.

Marisa found the book she'd been reading and made herself comfortable in an easy chair. Later that afternoon, there was another knock at her door.

Cliff ran up the hallway from the kitchen to the door and swung the door open. "It's a big guy, Marisa."

"Thanks, Cliff," Marisa said, reaching the door and glancing from the boy to the man in her doorway. "Mr.

Ramon. This is a surprise." She stiffened her spine and
firmed her jaw. She turned to Cliff at her side. "I'll take
care of this, Cliff. You can go back to your art project."

"Okay," he said, turning and walking away slowly.

Marisa looked at Lee. "Was there something you
wanted?"

"Most definitely."

"What is it?"

"I want to apologize, Marisa. I shouldn't have kept
who I am a secret." He slid his fingers through his short,
dark hair. "May I come in?"

She opened the door a little wider and stepped aside.

Lee entered her domain, and a familiar, unexplainable
spark of magic came with him.

Marisa closed the door, moved away from him a bit
and folded her arms.

"I wasn't purposely trying to hide anything, Marisa.
For some reason, things seemed out of the realm of nor-
mal in that elevator this morning."

She knew what he meant.

"You seemed rather nervous over our predicament, and
you had every right to be. When you made it clear you
weren't too happy with the new owner of the building, I
was afraid if I told you who I was it might do more harm
than good at the time."

Marisa shook her head. "You should have told me the
truth, Lee."

"You're right, Marisa. I was wrong. I apologize."

Marisa opened her mouth to respond, but the only
sound that filled the apartment was the squeak of an un-
tuned piano. Marisa spun around. "Cliff. That piano
needs tuning, sport. You'll have to play it another time."

"Not while I'm here," Lee said, striding toward the piano. "Have you got pliers, a screw driver, a hammer and a couple of peanut butter sandwiches?" Lee called to Marisa over his shoulder.

Marisa caught up with Lee at the piano. "What?"

"If I'm going to tune this piano, I'll need some tools, won't I?"

"You know how to fix pianos?" Cliff asked.

"Humph," Marisa said, folding her arms defiantly. "Sounds to me from the tools he requested more like he knows how to unfix pianos."

"Don't you believe me?" Lee asked, grinning down at her.

She shook her head. "No."

"Get the tools and the sandwiches, and we'll see who's right."

"But what are the sandwiches for? You aren't going to spread peanut butter all over my piano, are you?"

Cliff giggled.

Lee scooped the first-grade graduate into his arms. "This little fella and I are hungry, right, buddy?"

"Right," Cliff said, giving an exaggerated nod.

Marisa couldn't help but smile at the odd picture of the two men in her apartment. Her stubborn resolve melted away. "Tools and sandwiches coming up."

When she'd prepared the sandwiches and added a couple of glasses of milk to the supplies Lee had requested, she delivered her goods.

Lee thanked her. "Cliff and I can take things on our own from here. We wouldn't want to keep you from whatever you were doing."

Marisa looked at him skeptically at first. But Cliff joined Lee in asking her to trust them to work on their own, and she complied. It had been a long time since Cliff had spent any time with a man, eighteen months to be exact. If Lee made the boy happy, if he could fill a void in the child's life for even a few moments, she wasn't going to interfere. She walked to the easy chair a few feet from the piano and picked up the book she'd placed on the table next to it. "I'll be in the bedroom reading."

Lee glanced at her and nodded before turning back to Cliff.

Inside her room, Marisa sat on the bed and tried to read, but she couldn't concentrate on her book. The sounds from the living room were far too intriguing to let her think of anything but what was happening in her home.

Cliff would ask a question, Lee would give an answer. A milk glass clanged, a boy's voice was stifled with a mouthful of peanut butter, a man tinkered with a hopelessly lost musical instrument.

What on earth would he use a hammer for on a piano? If the instrument was worth more than the garbage fee it would cost to haul it away, Marisa would be worried about what Lee was doing to the valueless hunk of wood.

The sounds of more tinkering alternated with a child's voice asking, "Is it done yet?"

Marisa giggled every time Cliff repeated his mantra. "Is it done yet?"

Lee didn't know what he'd gotten himself into. It served him right.

Marisa's only worry was that Cliff would be terribly disappointed when the piano still sounded like squeaky pipes after Lee finished his tune up.

"Is it done yet?" Marisa heard for the umpteenth time.

"Yes," Lee finally replied. "Let me test it first, then you can play."

Marisa got off the bed and went to the door. She prepared herself for the worst rendition of *Chopsticks* she'd ever heard. But when the music started, the sound that startled her was Beethoven's *Moonlight Sonata*. She swung open the door and opened her mouth to speak.

"Let me try," Cliff said, scooting up against Lee.

Now was not the time to ask Lee how he got such sweet sounds out of an old rusty can. This was Cliff's moment. Marisa wasn't about to steal something so precious from a little boy who'd suffered more from the loss of a father than any child should suffer.

Marisa went back to her bed and sat and listened. Lee began to teach Cliff a real song. She didn't know the name of it but that didn't matter. All that counted was that Cliff was enjoying himself.

By the time Randi arrived, Cliff had become proficient in the notes Lee had taught him. After introductions were made, Cliff showed Randi how well he could play his new song. "Lee told me he would teach me another song on our piano if I wanted him to, but I told him we don't have a piano, Mom."

"No, Lee, I'm afraid we don't, but I do appreciate you teaching Cliff this song on Marisa's piano."

Cliff looked up at Marisa as the four of them stood gathered around the piano. "Would it be all right if Lee gave me more lessons on your piano, Marisa?"

She glanced from Cliff to Lee to Randi.

Randi lifted her boy and placed him on her hip. "We'll talk about that tomorrow. Right now we need to go home. I'm very tired. I've got laundry to do, and you, young man, need a bath."

Cliff struggled out of Randi's arms. He went to Lee and

stuck out his hand. "Thanks for showing me how to play the piano, Lee."

"My pleasure, buddy," Lee said, smiling at the boy and shaking his hand.

Next Cliff offered his hand to Marisa. "Thanks for the peanut butter sandwich, Marisa."

Marisa shook Cliff's hand. "Anytime."

Randi scooped Cliff back into her arms. "Good-bye. Thanks both of you."

"Our pleasure." Lee and Marisa spoke in unison.

When Randi let herself out the door, Lee and Marisa looked at each other tentatively.

Our pleasure? Marisa repeated mentally. They'd said it as though they were a couple, and this was their home. Worse yet, the second they'd uttered the words, they seemed right and natural. Marisa moved her head in order to dislodge the inappropriate thoughts that shook her equilibrium.

"I'd better be going," Lee said slowly. "We're alright now on my lack of being up front with you this morning, aren't we?"

"Of course, but I do have something I'd like to discuss with you, Lee."

"What I intend to do with the building?"

"Right." Marisa waved her hand toward the sofa. "Would you like to sit down?"

"Thank you," he said, motioning for her to sit first.

Marisa made herself comfortable at one end of the sofa while Lee sat near the other end.

A thick silence hung in the air. Before Marisa began, she cleared her throat. "Are you going to evict us?"

Lee's eyebrows lifted a moment, then settled where they belonged over his warm, brown eyes. He sat forward, looking a little uncomfortable. "Frankly, I don't want to evict anyone. I'd like for the current tenants to stay on and buy their apartments."

"Suppose we can't?"

He leaned back and studied her carefully. "Those who don't contract to buy their apartments will have to leave."

"How very succinct." Marisa took a deep breath and let it out slowly. "I guess that's it then. We'll all have to go." She looked at him, wondering how he could stand being in a business that took homes away from people. Then she said, "You're going to make this building a place for the wealthy, aren't you?"

Lee straightened in his seat. He softened his expression and stared at Marisa. "No, I'm not."

"You're not going to turn this building into condos?"

"Not for the rich." He turned toward her and laid his arm on the back of the sofa. "Marisa, did you know that in the United States most family incomes fall into the middle-income range?"

"Sure."

"Economic success in this country depends on those people. They do most of the buying. They do most of the working. Businesses make huge profits from these middle-income families. You don't have to sell to the rich to make money."

Marisa frowned at him. "What does this economics lesson have to do with anything?"

"My dream for this building is to turn it into homes for middle-income families and singles."

"Because you can make profits from them just like you make profits from the rich."

"Exactly."

"And business is all about profits."

Lee shrugged. "It's what makes the world go round."

Marisa eyed him suspiciously. "Some have said it is love and not money that makes the world go round."

He smiled at her. "Maybe it's both, but when it comes right down to it, it isn't love that puts a roof over someone's head. It's money."

"My point exactly. Is the roof over my head going to have to change?"

Lee moved to the edge of the sofa. "That depends on you, Marisa," he said, rising to his feet. "I'm an investor and a general contractor. I've got a job to do, a building to renovate, people to put to work."

She stood and listened to his explanation.

"I hope you and all the other tenants who want to stay will purchase your apartments. The price will be fair to both of us, and," he said, widening his eyes as he spoke, "you have to admit I've already made some excellent improvements to the building."

"You mean fixing the leaks?"

"Yes, repairing the leaks in the windows and the roof, fixing the holes in the walls in the hallways, getting rid of the rodent problem in the basement, sprucing up the unattended plants in the outdoor sitting area, renovating the broken playground equipment, constructing the picnic area in the back, building the gazebo, securing the loose bricks on the north side of the building and making a few other improvements as well."

She bit her lip. "I admit you've made some wonderful improvements so far."

Lee grinned. "Thank you."

"Making repairs is making improvements, but putting

people out of their homes doesn't improve real estate or better the community."

"Whether or not you want to believe me, Marisa, I really don't want to evict anyone. I truly hope all my tenants will stay on and purchase their apartments." He paused, staring at her thoughtfully. "If they can't," he added, shrugging, "they can't."

Marisa waved her hand toward her front door. "At least I understand your position. Thanks for making yourself clear."

They walked to the door together.

Lee turned around to face her before he let himself out. "And your understanding is?"

"That you are a businessman, one hundred percent. Profits come before anything else. If we can't line your pockets with real estate gold, we'll have to give up our homes."

He reacted to her words as though she'd viciously slapped him in the face but she continued.

"When you come up with a dollar figure for the purchase of my apartment, let me know. I'm sure it will be out of my budget, but I'd like to know it anyway."

He nodded slowly, thoughtfully. "I'll speak to you in a few days."

"Fine."

He opened the door.

"Lee."

He turned back to look at her.

"Thanks for spending time with Cliff. He has missed spending time with a man since his father died. It was real nice of you to be so kind to him."

He gave her a warm, half smile. "It was my pleasure. He's a great kid."

Marisa bit her lip and nodded. "He is. It'll be hard on him to lose his home."

The grin on Lee's face was instantly replaced by the slapped-in-the-mouth expression he'd shown Marisa a moment before. He turned and walked out of her apartment.

Chapter Three

Lee heard the door shut behind him. He stood in the hall outside Marisa's apartment without moving. This job was not going to be an easy one.

The other buildings Lee had purchased were abandoned. He had never had to evict anyone.

The deal had looked so simple on paper. Lee felt he was buying just another building. Apartment dwellers were mobile. They could move if they didn't want to buy the new condos. He had never even considered that renters might think of their apartments as real homes. If people wanted homes, they bought houses or condos, they didn't rent.

Before meeting Marisa, Lee had seen his tenants as objects which may either get in the way of his investment or become a part of its success when they purchased their condos.

Lee glanced back at Marisa's door. He couldn't let her get to him. Business was business. Everyone knew that. Renters know their tenancy is subject to change. If they wanted something more permanent, they should buy homes instead of rent them.

He looked ahead and firmed his resolve. He had taken on investors this time. He owed the profits he had promised to his partners. He couldn't afford to grow a soft-hearted attitude. If his tenants had to move, they had to move. It wouldn't kill a single one of them. He had a job to do, and, by heaven, he was going to do it.

Lee glanced back at Marisa's apartment one more time as he started to walk forward. Suddenly, he felt something soft on his chest. His gaze snapped from Marisa's door to Cliff's mother.

"Oh, excuse me, Lee," Randi said.

He took hold of the basket of laundry she was carrying. "It's my fault, Randi. I wasn't looking where I was going."

She ran a hand through her disheveled blond hair. "Actually, I'm glad I have a chance to talk to you again. I wanted to express my gratitude for you taking the time to teach my son a little something about playing the piano. He talked about it nonstop. It wasn't easy to get him to settle down for his bath."

Lee smiled. "You've got a great kid, Randi."

She released a tired sigh. "He's great, but he's a handful. It isn't easy being a single mother. That's why I appreciate it so much when someone else helps me out the way you did today."

He waved a nonchalant hand. "It was my pleasure." He took a breath before he went on. "And I'm sorry about your husband's passing, ma'am."

She lifted her chin. "I guess Marisa told you."

"Yes."

"Mac was a carpenter. A great carpenter. We had our own business. I helped him with his work from time to time, but I wasn't there the day he . . ." She looked away and wiped her eyes.

Lee swallowed hard when her words began to sound too familiar. "He was killed in an accident at work?" he asked slowly.

She nodded. "He was working on a roof. His safety harness was defective." Tears rolled down her cheeks. She looked away. "He left a lot of bills. Cliff and I lost our house . . ." Randi wiped both of her hands over her face and looked at Lee. She pushed her lips into a smile that could only be forced. "I'm so sorry. All I wanted to do was thank you and explain why your kindness to Cliff meant so much to me. I didn't mean to go on about my troubles."

Lee shifted the basket of laundry to one hip. He gripped Randi's shoulder with his hand. "No problem." He gave her a smile he hoped brought her comfort as well. "Would you like me to take this laundry inside your apartment for you."

Randi reached for the basket. "Don't be silly. I'm fine." She glanced at her watch. "I'd better get going before Cliff gets himself into trouble of some sort." She gave Lee an inquisitive expression. "Why is it that seven-year-old boys are such experts at getting into trouble?"

Lee smiled. "I'm afraid I don't know anything about that. I don't have kids."

Randi took a deep breath and exhaled. "Well, if you ever find the answer, let me know." She turned and let herself into her apartment.

Lee leaned against the wall. When Randi had told him her husband had died in a construction accident it brought memories of Stock Reed. He rubbed his stomach to squelch the churning. "Just like Stock," Lee whispered.

Stock's accident had been Lee's fault. Maybe not technically or legally, but Lee blamed himself just the same. He shouldn't have driven his men so hard, but he had a deadline to meet. Time was money. If Lee hadn't insisted the men finish work on the front façade of that building before the end of the day, Stock would not have fallen to his death.

Stock had a family too, a wife as pretty as Randi and twin girls. They had lost Stock, but at least they were well provided for financially. Lee had seen to that.

Randi, on the other hand, had been wearing a waitress uniform when she came into Marisa's apartment earlier. The jeans and T-shirt she wore in the hall had seen better days.

She would never be able to buy her new condo. If she had bills she was struggling to pay from her husband's business, chances are her credit would never be good enough to get a loan for the condo even if she could afford the payments.

Lee rubbed his belly again. He cleared his head and tried to take his mind off Randi and Cliff. He couldn't get involved in people's personal lives.

He stood up straight and steadied his legs. As he was about to walk forward, Hal Bristo rounded the corner and pinned Lee right where he stood. The burly, fifty-five-year-old man had a gaze as sharp as a bolt of lightning.

Great, Lee thought, just what he needed, a man who hated him. "Hal," Lee said amiably, "what can I do for you?"

"You can tell me what the heck is going on."

Lee took a step forward. "Why don't we go up to my apartment and talk?"

"We'll talk right here." Fire burned in Hal's eyes. His

jaw looked as hard as iron. The paunchy man tugged his belt up over his belly.

"I really think it would be better if we went to my apartment. We shouldn't disturb the tenants." Lee began to wonder if he'd ever get out of the hallway.

"I don't care two hoots for the tenants," Hal said, staring at Lee, challenging him to a showdown.

Lee gave back what he got. His gaze bore into Hal like a laser cutting metal. "Let's keep it short and quiet. Whether you care about the tenants or not, they do have the right to peace and quiet."

Hal glared at Lee a moment longer, then gave him a hard nod. "Alright."

Lee shoved his hands into his pockets. "What's the problem this time?"

"Talk is that you're planning to hire some of the scabs that worked for you on your last project."

Lee's spine turned into iron. His jaw became as firm as granite, and he spoke his words very deliberately.

"Don't ever use that term around me. My former crew were hard working people, the hardest working I've ever seen. They were good men and women. I'd have brought them along with me on this project if I could have."

Hal took on a sinister grin. "Couldn't though, could you? Your partners don't like scabs working on their building, only union people."

Lee clenched his fists inside his pockets and used every ounce of strength he possessed to keep his hands right where they were—no matter how much he wanted to let his fists wipe the grin off Hal's face. "I don't know where you got your information, but I'm not hiring any new workers, Bristo." He pulled his hands from his pocket and folded his arms across his chest. "Anything else?"

Hal shifted his weight, stretched up and tried unsuccessfully to match Lee's height. He eyed Lee intently in a showdown of wills. "Nothing else. I just wanted to let you know that there will be no scabs working on this project. You keep that last crew of scabs of yours and all other people that don't belong working here away from this building, got it?"

Lee grabbed Hal by the collar. "I told you not to use that word," he said through gritted teeth.

Hal covered his face with a nasty grin. "Touchy about your crew, huh?"

Lee let go of Hal's collar. He stood back and wiped his hand over his mouth.

"Bet it's hard for you to even show your face on another construction project after the way you blew the last one you worked on. Lost a few million on that one didn't you?"

"Bristo," Lee said, willing himself not to punch his crew foreman, "get back to work."

Hal nodded. "In a minute."

"Now, or you're fired," Lee growled.

"Fired?" Hal laughed. "You know you can't fire me. We're stuck with each other. Your investors saw to that." He looked Lee up and down. "But I will tell you this. If I had known I was going to be working for L. C. Ramon, the man who hires scabs to work his projects, who lost millions on his last project, the man who was responsible for the death of—"

Lee grabbed Hal by the collar and shook him. The foreman went too far when he started to talk about Stock Reed.

Hal brought locked hands up against Lee's belly, right under his ribs.

Lee instantly released his grasp on Hal and fell back when the wind left his lungs. He hit the wall. As he started to get up, fire under his ribs, anger coursing through his veins, a fist clenched and ready to shove the smirk off Hal's face, he heard a door open.

"Stop it!" Marisa ordered. "Stop all this noise right now!"

Lee looked at her as he stood and wiped a hand over his mouth.

"Just a little misunderstanding, ma'am," Hal said in a voice dripping with false remorse.

Lee looked at his foreman and made a mental note to remember what a good actor Hal could be, how quickly he could change his mood. He glanced back at Marisa. "He's right," Lee said, "just a misunderstanding."

Marisa folded her arms. "Humph. Your misunderstanding has blood dripping all over the hallway," she said, looking up at Lee.

Lee glanced down at his arm. A gash spewed blood over his clothes and the wood floor of the hallway. He must have hit a nail sticking out of the wall on his way to the floor. He looked back at Marisa. "Guess I cut it when I fell."

"Yeah, you'd better watch your step, Ramon," Hal said in an even tone.

Lee gave Hal a stern look. "I guess I'd better," he replied, using the same tone Hal had used.

Marisa reached toward Lee and took his hand. "Come inside with me. I'll clean you up, then we'll clean up this mess in the hall."

Hal cleared his throat. "Sorry for the disturbance, ma'am."

Marisa scowled at him. "Don't let it happen again." She looked from Hal to Lee and back at the paunchy foreman again. "Either one of you."

Hal jerked his chin and tugged his belt up over his belly. "See you in 3-E in an hour," he said, blazing dark eyes in Lee's direction. He stared at his boss a moment longer, then he turned and walked away.

Marisa tugged at Lee's hand. "Come on, slugger. Let's go inside and get that bleeding to stop."

Lee took a deep breath and turned to follow Marisa. He pushed her apartment door open for her. Once they were inside, he shoved the door shut with his foot as Marisa dragged him toward the kitchen. When they reached her sink, he pulled his hand away from her. "I can take care of myself."

She let him clean his wound.

He looked away so she couldn't see the face that surely reflected the pain the running water caused his cut.

"I have some antibiotic cream," she said softly. She stepped close to Lee and touched his arm. "Can I see it?"

He had intended to pull his arm away from her, but her touch was so warm and comforting, it compelled him to show her his injury.

She looked at it, then she lifted her eyes to meet his gaze. "I think you might need a couple of stitches."

Lee stared down at her. She was so pretty. He wanted to cup her cheek in his hand and touch her sweet skin.

"Should I take you to the hospital?" Marisa asked.

Lee blinked and broke the hold she had on him. "What? The hospital? What for?"

"The stitches." She studied his wound again. "I think you'll need at least two stitches." She reached for the paper towels and tore off a couple of sheets. She wadded them up and applied them to Lee's cut.

Lee put his hand over hers. "I can do this myself."

She tugged her hand away. "Okay," she said, stepping back.

He pressed the ball of paper tight against his arm. "I don't need stitches. I've had cuts like this hundreds of times. I'll get the bleeding to stop, put some of that cream on it as you suggested and slap a bandage over it. It'll heal in no time."

She eyed him a moment very carefully, and Lee wished he had some inkling of what was going through her mind as she perused him.

"I'll go get the antibiotic cream and bandages," Marisa said, backing away.

Lee nodded and watched her go towards the bathroom. When she was out of sight, he lifted the paper towel and checked his cut. The bleeding had stopped. He washed the wound with soap and water, biting back the expletives he wanted to spew when the water hit his injury.

When Marisa came back to him, he was drying his arm with a fresh paper towel.

"Let me see that," Marisa said, taking Lee's arm. Her gentle touch sent tingles up to his shoulder. She shook her head and looked up at him. "I think you should get stitches."

Lee took hold of her chin with his free hand so he could compel her to look at him instead of his cut. "Marisa, I've been working construction for twenty years, ever since I was fourteen years old. I've seen dozens of injuries. I don't need stitches."

She let go of his arm and pulled away from him. "If you say so."

"I do." He took the antibiotic cream and squeezed the tube, laying a line of cream over his cut. He bit his lip to subdue his pain. Then he placed a bandage over his wound.

"Finished?" Marisa asked.

He glanced at her. "Nothing to it. Thanks for the first aid."

"No problem." She lifted her chin. "Now that your injury is taken care of and you're alright, I have a few things to say to you." Her entire demeanor changed. She no longer looked like a helpful angel. She looked a lot more like a very upset woman.

Lee felt his brows creeping toward each other. "What?" he asked, puzzled by her change in attitude.

She folded her arms. "What is the matter with you and that hulk in the hallway? Why were you fighting? This is a respectable building. We don't have fistfights in the halls."

Lee took a deep breath and tried to figure out where her hostility was coming from. She was as gentle as an angel a moment before. "We weren't having a fistfight. We had a little disagreement. I stumbled over my own feet and fell."

"Naturally," she said sarcastically. "I'm sure you're falling over your feet all the time."

She knew he was lying. The fact was, if she hadn't intervened when she did, Lee's blood wouldn't have been the only blood spilled out in that hall. He straightened up and collected himself. "I'm not going to discuss what was going on with you. You have a right to be angry that we disturbed you. I'll accept your complaint and offer my apologies."

She studied him for a moment, then she said, "Apology accepted, but you'd better watch your feet. You wouldn't want to fall again."

She took a step forward and the next thing Lee knew, Marisa was falling into him. He caught her and held her close.

She stared up at him, her dark green eyes deep and full of surprise. "Sorry about that," Marisa said, pulling herself back.

Lee looked at her for a moment, then he began to smile. "Guess I'm not the only one who falls over his own feet."

Marisa glanced at the floor. She bent down to pick up a handful of crayons. She stood and held them up for Lee to see. "Cliff left a bunch of his art supplies on the floor."

"Okay," Lee said, "so I'm the only one of the two of us that is a klutz."

Marisa shook her head and looked at him thoughtfully. "You're no klutz, Lee Charles Ramon. Don't think for one minute that I buy your story about falling over your own feet." She folded her arms across her chest and took a deep breath. "No good ever comes from fighting."

Lee reflected on her advice. "You're right."

The look on her face told him she was surprised to hear him agree with her. But then she looked puzzled.

"I'm sorry for the disturbance." He glanced toward the sink, then back at her. "If I could borrow a bucket and some wash rags or paper towels, I'll clean up the mess I made in the hall. If I could borrow your hammer again, I'll take care of that nail sticking out of the wall that must have caused my cut."

She took hold of his arm. "Lee, you scared me."

"What?" It was his turn to be surprised.

"When I heard the shouting in the hall and the thud of your body hitting the floor . . . it scared me." She looked away then back at him. "When I saw you were bleeding. . . ."

He covered the hand she had put on his arm and gazed back at her. "I had no idea . . . I never thought . . . I'm sorry."

"I know," she said softly as she squeezed his arm. "I'm glad you're alright." She pulled her hand from him. "I'll get a bucket of water so we can clean up the hall."

Lee took hold of her hand. "I am truly sorry, Marisa. It won't happen again."

She nodded. "I believe you."

He let go of her hand. It never occurred to him that the threat of violence in her hallway would frighten Marisa, especially when it had nothing to do with her. He suddenly felt like the biggest heel on the planet.

"I'll get the hammer and cleaning supplies," Marisa said. "You take some paper towels and wipe up the blood on my floor and in the hall. I have a cleaning product to get the blood stains out of the carpet in my living room. You can borrow it to get the stains off your shirt. We'll wash the floors." Marisa went to her bathroom to get the supplies.

Lee looked at the blood he had shed all over her apartment. What a nuisance he had made of himself. Marisa had every right to scream at him and kick his backside out of her apartment and all the way down the hall. But she didn't. She had given him a well-deserved scolding, but mostly, she'd treated him with kindness, and now she was even going to help him tidy up his mess.

He shook his head and stared towards Marisa. She was an amazing woman, and he had to get to know her better.

Chapter Four

The next few days, Lee worked fifteen hours a day with his union crew converting apartments 3-E and 3-F from a two-bedroom and efficiency unit into a three-bedroom apartment. His investors wanted results as soon as possible. Lee couldn't afford to lose a nickel on this project, and, since he was working as the general contractor for the renovation, he was financially responsible if the job wasn't finished on time. But he would also reap the rewards before the other investors if the project was completed ahead of schedule. Working long days would be worth every aching muscle and hour of lost sleep.

Late one evening, Randi Jarvis quietly came into apartment 3-E as Lee worked alone taping and mudding Sheetrock in the unit's living room.

"Lee, may I speak with you?"

Lee set down the tape he was holding and walked over to Randi. "Of course. It wouldn't be very neighborly of me to turn you down," he said, smiling at her.

She forced a smile. "Glad to hear it, but, as for us being neighbors, I'm afraid that won't last long. That's what I came to see you about."

Lee didn't like what he saw in Randi's eyes. He recognized pain, and he didn't like seeing it in this frail woman. He glanced at the newly-remodeled kitchen area of the apartment. When he looked back at Randi, he waved his arm toward the counter that divided the kitchen from the dining area. "Would you like to sit and have a cup of coffee with me? I could really use a break."

Randi looked nervously toward the front door. "I guess I could," she said, turning back to Lee. "Cliff's asleep. I don't like to leave him alone, but he should be alright as long as he's sleeping."

Lee took off his hard hat and tossed it next to the bucket of mud he had been putting on the walls. He ran his hands through his hair and over his clothes to clean up a little. He was pretty dirty from working his fifteen-hour day. "How do you take your coffee?" he asked his companion.

"Any way you take it is fine with me. I'm not particular."

He led her to the counter and held a swivel stool for her as she sat down. Then he walked to the sink and washed himself up. He poured coffee into two paper cups. "I made this a couple of hours ago," he said, coming around the counter and sitting next to Randi on a stool. "I hope it isn't too ripe for you."

Randi gave him a soft chuckle as she took the cup. "I'm sure it's fine." She tasted his concoction and made a face at him. "It's awful."

Lee laughed, sipped from his cup and agreed with her. "Good thing I'm not a restaurateur."

"If you were, I think *coffeehouses* would be safe."

Lee chuckled again and agreed.

Randi smiled, reached toward Lee and touched his arm. "Don't worry, Lee. I've had worse than this," she said, lifting her cup. "As I told you, I used to work with Mac on his projects. The coffee construction workers make can get pretty bad."

He nodded and said, "I'm living proof of that."

She acknowledged his comment with another smile. Then she took a sip of his coffee, grimaced and set her cup on the counter. "Those were the days," she said with a sigh. "Mac was a carpenter, but he did all kinds of renovations in addition to those that required his carpentry skills. I've helped him drywall, paint, lay vinyl, tile and wood floors and carpets, hang ceilings, put up woodwork, even hang doors."

"Very impressive." She amazed Lee with her knowledge of remodeling. She was so frail looking, he would never have expected her to have done such physical work. Not that waitressing was not physical. It was. But it couldn't be as physically demanding as putting Sheetrock on a ceiling. "Maybe I should hire you to work for me."

Randi chuckled and took a sip of coffee. She grimaced again and pushed the cup aside. "I don't think so," she said, shaking her head. "I heard a little of the conversation between you and your foreman. He doesn't have a very high opinion of non-union laborers."

Guilt stirred in Lee's stomach. He had hoped Randi had not heard what had gone on between him and Hal in the hallway a few days ago. "I'm sorry about that, Randi."

She waved a hand nonchalantly. "Forget it. I was just about to come out in the hall and level the guy for what he was saying about non-union workers when I heard a big thud. I had hoped you had decked him yourself, but that's not what I heard from Marisa." She took a deep breath and glanced at the bandage on his arm. "Is your cut healing okay?"

Lee looked at his injury then focused on Randi again. "So the news has traveled all over the building, huh?"

Randi shook her head. "Marisa isn't like that. We live across the hall from each other. We're friends. I asked her what had happened when I saw her the next day. She filled me in, but I don't think she mentioned the incident to anyone else."

"I hope not. I do regret what happened."

Randi put her elbow on the counter and laid her head in her hand. "It wasn't your fault. Mac and I had our share of guys like your foreman to deal with. That type corners you and pushes all the right buttons to trap you into doing exactly what he wants."

Lee took a drink of coffee. "Oh, that's bad," he said, pushing his cup away. "You're right about Hal. He is that kind of guy, but that's no excuse for me letting it happen. I'm sorry to have disturbed you and Marisa. It won't happen again."

Randi shrugged and sighed. "For your sake, I hope it doesn't. I like you, and I don't want to see you get hurt. But as for me, it really doesn't matter. I'm looking for a new place to live. I won't be able to buy my apartment, as much as I'd love to do just that. I miss owning my home, but I've still got too many bills left from our business. I've got to square things with my creditors before I can invest in a new home."

Lee's insides began to churn. "I'm sorry, Randi. If there was any other way, I'd give you a break, but—"

She held a hand in the air. "Don't. I understand. It's business. You've got to watch the bottom line."

"That's right." Lee felt like a big jerk. "You don't have to move right away."

She took a deep breath and exhaled slowly. "This is going to be real tough on Cliff. He loves it here, and he's made friends with some of the children in the neighborhood. I think the sooner we find an apartment, the better it will be for Cliff. Knowing for a couple of months that he was going to have to leave his friends would be harder on him than just up and leaving them." She glanced away a moment then looked back at him. "I'll bring him back to visit once in a while."

Lee could barely stand to look at the pain in Randi's eyes. He wanted to look away, but he didn't want to treat her with anything that she might see as disrespect. "Maybe you could get a second job to earn the down payment on the condo. If you could put a good-sized down payment together, the payments probably wouldn't be any higher than the rent you pay now. Interest rates are real low."

Randi looked down at the counter and brushed away a line of construction dust. She shook her head and lifted her gaze back to Lee. "I already spend too much time away from Cliff. If I took on another job, we'd never have any time together. Besides, it's summer. Cliff's not in school. Most of the extra money I'd earn would go for baby-sitting."

"Maybe you could find something where you could take Cliff along while you work." He was grasping at straws. He knew that, but he wanted to help this woman. He liked her. She was the widow of a brother construction worker like Stock Reed.

She smiled at him and shook her head. "That's not going to happen," she said as she slipped off her stool.

Lee left his stool and accepted the fact that Randi was

right. She wouldn't find an employer who would welcome a woman's son in the workplace, and she had no choice but to find a new place to live. But that only made Lee feel guilty. It was his fault that she had to leave her home. It was as though he was hurting the wife of his dear friend Stock. Randi even looked like Helen Reed.

Lee slipped his hand to the small of Randi's back. "If there's anything I can do to help, let me know, will you?"

"Other than letting me out of my lease a little early when I find a new place, there's nothing you or anyone can do, Lee. You're just doing your job trying to earn a living renovating this old building. I'm doing my job trying to take care of myself and my son the best I can." She stopped short and looked around the apartment under construction. "I've got to admit seeing all this renovation work going on makes me miss helping Mac with his work. I really liked it, you know. I was good at it, too. If I didn't have to take care of Cliff all alone, I'd work in this profession again. As it is, I wouldn't have the stamina to work construction all day, day after day, year-round and come home to face all the tasks of parenting and maintaining a household by myself."

"You miss construction work? You would do it full time if you could?"

She nodded. "I sure would."

"And you really did all the things you mentioned earlier, dry walling, painting, laying flooring?"

"Many times. I used to take Cliff with me since it was Mac's projects I was working on."

"I wonder . . ."

"What?"

"When I suggested before that you work for me, I only half meant it."

"Because of the union men."

"Yes. I agreed to use only union people on this project. I hate narrowing my scope of workers like that because I like to give everyone a fair shot. But I was between a rock and a hard place, which I won't get into with you." Lee hesitated a moment before he finished his thought. He rubbed his hand over his jaw. "Did you and your husband work in housing or commercial buildings?"

"Housing."

"Then you are familiar with sweat equity, aren't you?"

"Sure."

Lee rubbed his fingers over his jaw again. "Would you like to do the renovations in your own apartment to earn your down payment?"

Randi's eyes turned into silver-blue moons. "Are you kidding?"

"I'm completely serious." Lee folded his arms over his chest. "Naturally, I'd have to have my licensed electricians and plumbers do the wiring, piping and heating, but you could do as much of the rest of the remodeling as you'd like. You can follow a set of plans, can't you?"

"Sure," she said enthusiastically. "But what about the union agreement you have?"

Lee waved a hand. "Forget that. You would be working on your own property. Technically, I wouldn't be hiring you. You would be working on the home you intended to buy. You're the home owner working on her own condo. That is a separate situation from anything I agreed to about using only union personnel." Lee rather liked the idea of getting the better of Hal. If he could help Randi and irritate his annoying foreman all at the same time, what would be the harm?

"And I could work and keep track of Cliff at the same time."

"Yes, you could."

Randi lunged toward Lee and threw her arms around his neck. She kissed him on the cheek, then let him go. "Thanks, Lee. You're a great guy. First piano lessons for Cliff, now saving our home."

Lee shifted uncomfortably. He was also the reason they had been in danger of losing their home in the first place. "I haven't saved anything for you yet, Randi. We'll have to take a look at the cost of your condo, figure out how much equity you can earn by working on the renovations yourself and make sure you can set up the financing. If you've had a lot of bills . . ."

She smiled at him. "I'm not behind on any of them, Lee. My credit is just fine. I've made sure of that."

He smiled. "I'm glad to hear that." He guided her to the door. "We'll get together in a couple of days and work things out. You take some time to think about what you're going to be getting yourself into, Randi. It won't be easy."

"But it will be worth it to stay where Cliff is so happy."

Lee nodded. "Whatever you say. I'll see you in a couple of days."

"Thanks, Lee. I won't let you down." She turned and left.

She won't let him down? He hoped he hadn't just put his foot in his mouth and set himself up to let her down. He had to give this sweat equity idea a good deal more thought. He couldn't afford to lose any money on this project. Before he met with Randi again to make plans, he had better crunch some numbers and make sure a sweat equity plan for her would be feasible.

Blast his unrestrained lips. He should not have spoken so impulsively.

* * *

The next day Lee was putting in an even longer day than the ones he had logged over the last few days. He watched his crew take down the wall between 3-E and 3-F for a few minutes, then he went to the counter. He poured himself a cup of coffee, commandeered the last donut in the box on the counter and ducked into the bedroom that had the stack of Sheetrock just high enough to sit on comfortably.

Staring out the window at the thick leaves of the ancient maple tree next to the building, Lee's thoughts turned to Marisa Orlando. She had impressed him immediately when they met in the elevator. Her thick, rust-colored hair and dark green eyes caught his attention first, but it was her feisty personality and her kindness that intrigued him most. He smiled as he imagined the small-framed woman soundly handling thirteen-year-old boys who outsized her. He had meant it when he told her she had a tough job. And he appreciated her kindness when she took care of him after his confrontation in the hall with Hal.

She wasn't happy about Lee coming into her world and turning it upside down with his condo conversion, but she would have to learn to live with it. He had committed himself, the remainder of his once sizable fortune and the money of his investors, to renovating this building. He had responsibilities no one could make him forget. He had to admit, though, if anyone could make him forget his duties, it would be Marisa.

An indefinable special air surrounded her. Her mere presence filled Lee with emotions he didn't understand. He felt whole when he was with her, like a winner. He desperately needed his confidence back. He had spent too many hours, weeks, months feeling like a failure since his last job. He had made so many mistakes and miscalcula-tions. Fortunately, it was only *his* own money he had lost and no one else's. But he had lost almost all that he had.

Lee finished the last of his coffee and crushed his paper cup in his hand.

His mistakes had cost more than money. They had cost Stock Reed his life.

Lee threw his crushed cup into the corner and walked to the window. He stared at the maple tree that stood in its spot for the last hundred years.

How he had wished time and again that he could relive the last two years. Everything had gone so wrong. It was as though someone had set out to sabotage all of his ef-forts. But there was no one to blame for his failures but himself.

Lee rubbed his hand over his face. He didn't feel like a failure when he was with Marisa. He had no idea why. They weren't even friends. As a matter of fact, she didn't like him. He was pretty sure she would be happy to have never met him since he intended to take away her home if she couldn't buy it herself.

He shoved his hands in his pockets and looked down as he headed around the Sheetrock for the door. He would have to stay out of the personal lives of his tenants, even Marisa. He couldn't get emotionally involved with any of them, especially Marisa, or he could be destroying him-self financially. He needed these apartments sold or va-cated so they could be sold as soon as he could see to the arrangements.

Lee reached the doorway of the bedroom and went through to the living area, vowing to keep his distance from all of his tenants. It would make it a lot easier to is-sue any necessary eviction notices when the time demanded it if he didn't think of the tenants as people who were losing their homes. Instead, he needed to think of them as pawns standing in the way of his success, his urgently-needed success.

"Am I intruding?"

Lee's gaze darted from the crew to the direction from where he heard her voice. "Marisa. No, you're not intruding. What can I do for you?"

She walked towards him slowly. "I'm sorry to interfere with your work, but I'm afraid I have a complaint."

Lee went over to Marisa. He took her arm and began to lead her to the bedroom with the Sheetrock. "Let's go in here. It won't be so loud, and we can talk." Inside the room Lee motioned toward the pile of drywall. "Have a seat. Tell me what's wrong."

Marisa didn't sit down. She swallowed hard and twisted a lock of copper hair in her finger. "Randi's apartment is just up the hall from here. Cliff goes to bed early. I'm afraid you may be keeping him awake with all the noise. If he doesn't get enough sleep, Randi can't get him up in the morning. Then she's late for work. She can't afford any trouble at work, Lee. She needs her job."

"When I knew we would be working late on this demolition, I checked with Randi. I figured she might not like us making so much noise since she had that little tyke to take care of. She told me about an hour ago that the noise wouldn't bother Cliff. It's only the apartment above them or the ones across the hall that can make enough noise to disturb Cliff's sleep."

Marisa inhaled deeply, "Lee, I'm sorry. I didn't mean to interfere. I thought I was helping out a friend."

Lee slipped his hand onto her lower back and guided her back out of the room. "No problem, but now that I have you here, I'm going to give you a chance to make up for jumping to conclusions."

He had to think fast to try to find a reason for Marisa to stay. Now that she was with him again, making him feel strong and successful, he didn't want to let her leave. He knew what he was feeling did not make any sense. But he also knew he wanted Marisa to stay, whether his reasons meant he was using good judgment or not.

Marisa looked up at him with a tentative smile. "What do you have in mind?"

"Have you ever done any remodeling work?"

"Me?" she asked. She shook her head. "Hardly."

"Why not?"

"Because I have no talent for it."

"Would you like to come into my world for a while, Marisa? I would like you to see what kind of work I do, what it feels like to transform an apartment, a home, an entire building into something new and wonderful without losing any of the architectural integrity."

Marisa waved her hand about her casually. "I don't think I could learn all that in a few minutes."

Lee lifted his chin and stroked his jaw with his fingers. "I see," he said, drawing out his words. "You're afraid."

Marisa briefly considered his challenge. "I'm not afraid of anything. All I wanted was to ask you to keep it quiet in case you might be disturbing Cliff. But, if you want me to help raise the noise level in this building, I'll give it a try."

"Splendid," he said, grinning at her.

"But I want you to know that I'm only doing this to show you that I'm not afraid of anything and to make up for accusing you falsely of being inconsiderate about disturbing the tenants. And because I was getting so bored in my apartment I was starting to read my cereal boxes."

Lee chuckled at her last reason. "That's pretty bored. I'm glad I could rescue you from an evening of reading cereal labels."

"You're a knight in shining armor," Marisa joked.

Lee grinned at her. "I'll get you a hard hat and a pair of safety glasses. You go into the other bedroom and I'll meet you in a few minutes. I'm taking down the plaster and lath in there so we can do some rewiring and any necessary repairs."

When Lee went to the second bedroom, he handed the supplies to Marisa. She took the hard hat and tucked her copper curls inside it as best she could. Then she put on the safety glasses.

Looking up at him, half hidden behind the safety glasses, Marisa was still a beautiful woman.

"What should I do?"

Lee looked around the work area. "If you think you could handle a shovel and a scraper, you could scrape plaster off the walls and load it into the wheelbarrow standing in the corner."

Marisa looked around the twelve by fifteen room. "I think I can manage that."

During the first hour, Marisa loaded refuse from the floor of the small room and hauled it down to the dumpster on the now fixed elevator. When she finished, she then worked closely with Lee removing plaster and loading it into the wheelbarrow.

Their interaction seemed intimate to Lee, as personal as watching a movie together or eating a meal at a fine restaurant. Lee knew his sense of their situation was foolish, but he couldn't help how he felt.

Hal Bristo entered their private world and shattered Lee's comfort. "Ma'am," he said to Marisa, "I'm the foreman on this job. I would like to see your union card."

Marisa tugged her safety glasses from her face. "I beg your pardon?"

Lee stepped next to Hal. "She's not union, Bristo, and she's not on the payroll. She's my . . ." He turned and looked at Marisa for a moment. When his gaze set on Bristo's menacing eyes once more, he said, "She's my intern. She wanted to learn a little about construction, and I'm teaching her."

"That's true," Marisa said, stepping next to Lee.

Hal looked from Lee to Marisa. "You're not getting paid?"

"No," Marisa said, removing her hat and letting her copper curls cascade over her shoulders. "I'm just having fun."

"Humph," Hal said, "if this is fun, you must be a bored woman."

Lee clenched his fist and readied himself to punch Hal in the mouth the way he should have a few days ago. A warm hand on his arm stopped him.

"Mr. Bristo, I'm a teacher. I love learning new things. I told Mr. Ramon that I've never worked on a remodeling project. He was kind enough to show me how a person begins to build a new room in an old building." She lifted the curls off her shoulders and gave her head a shake. "I think it's fascinating. You, Bristo, Mr. Ramon and your crew must love your work."

Hal grunted at her. "Yeah, we love it." He looked at Lee. "No funny business going on here then? She's not a scab?"

Lee clenched his fist again.

Marisa squeezed his arm. "Mr. Bristo, you have quite a knack for abusing words. The callous word you use, scab, refers to a person who works when union workers go on strike. Are you on strike, or is anyone else working on this building on strike?"

"No."

"Then that foul word has no place in this conversation. Even in what some might deem appropriate circumstances, the term 'scab' is always in bad taste when it refers to a human being." Before Hal could comment further, Marisa went on. "Besides, if Mr. Ramon were going to hire non-union workers, he could certainly find more qualified people than someone like me who'd never done more than paint a closet in the way of home improvement."

Hal folded his arms over his chest and muttered something unpleasant.

"Was there anything else you wanted, Mr. Bristo?" Marisa asked sweetly.

Hal looked at Lee. "It's ten-thirty. We're going home for the night. We'll be back at eight." He turned abruptly, but, before he could leave, Marisa called him back.

"Mr. Bristo?"

He turned to face her. "What?"

"Just so you know, I do belong to a union, a teachers' union."

He grunted at her and walked out of the apartment, slamming the door behind him.

Lee couldn't hold back his emotions any longer. He reached for Marisa and scooped her into his arms. He spun her around the room, being careful not to fall over the debris laying on the floor. "You're beautiful, Marisa. You cut that guy up with the blades of his own knife."

She pushed herself out of his embrace. "I did no such

thing. There are certain words I can't stand being used at all let alone being used improperly, even slang words. At the top of my list is irregardless. There is no such word. The proper word is regardless. Another word is infer. People will say, 'He told her the meat was overdone, inferring that she had burned it.' The proper word to use is *imply* in this case. With words like 'scab' in the sense that Mr. Bristo meant it, I just plain see red. I don't like any words that degrade human beings. Period. I just wanted to make a point."

Lee touched her chin and chuckled. "Well, that you did, Miss English Teacher, and you did it well. So well, it calls for a drink. I've got sodas in the fridge. Let's go have a drink." He put his arm around her shoulders and led her to the kitchen.

"I'm glad we have this time alone together, Lee. I have something to tell you. It's the real reason I agreed to stay when you asked me." She made herself comfortable on one of the stools while Lee got the sodas. "I took you up on your offer to help out for a while because I was hoping for an opening to bring up what I wanted to talk about. Since such an opportunity never arose, I'll just have to say what I have to say."

Lee took the seat next to her and handed her a soda. "So you didn't come to complain about the noise?"

Marisa popped open her soda and took a sip. "I did, yes, but not only for that reason. I have something else to discuss with you as well."

Lee sipped his soda and eyed her suspiciously. "I have the distinct feeling I'm not going to like this."

Marisa bit her lip and said, "You're probably right."

Chapter Five

"Might as well just say what you have to say," Lee said.

Marisa felt a knot growing in her belly, but she couldn't let that stop her. "I know we've talked about this before, but I just have to ask again." She took a deep breath and exhaled quickly. "Do you have to sell all the apartments? Isn't there any way we tenants could continue to rent from you?"

He looked away from her. When he turned toward her again, he rubbed his hand over his face and gazed into her eyes. "Marisa, I've told you we're renovating this building to sell the units as condos." He left his stool and walked to the sink. He washed his hands, then he turned back towards her. "Notices will be going to tenants tomorrow. They have sixty days to either move or buy their units." He folded his arms and leaned against the sink. "It's out of my hands."

"What?" she asked, not believing what he was saying. "What do you mean it's out of your hands?" She slid off her stool and walked towards him. "You're the one making us move out of our homes. Some of the tenants have lived here ten, fifteen or even more than twenty years. How can you just kick them out of their homes?"

He rubbed his hand over his face once more. "Let me explain things to you as best I can." He stared down at her, his dark brown eyes showing signs of apprehension which Marisa didn't expect to see. "I have investors. I'm not alone on this project. I have responsibilities. Even if I wanted to do as you ask, I couldn't. It wouldn't be fair to my partners. We've all invested a great deal of money in this project."

Marisa folded her arms in exasperation. "I hate money. I hate having to need it to survive. I hate having to lose it to pay bills to keep people we love from being sick or from dying. I hate never having enough of it, and I hate the way it makes people crave it like they do air or food."

Lee gave her an odd look, but then why shouldn't he? She was talking irrationally.

"Whatever your opinion of money is, it's a very necessary part of life, just as you admitted. It's also a major part of business. And business is business, Marisa. My partners and I haven't invested our time and money in this renovation for the fun of it. We're here to make a profit, and I think what we are doing is beneficial to people. This building needs lots of work. It's been neglected for far too long. If improvements weren't made, it would have been condemned within a couple of years anyway. Under those circumstances, the tenants would have had no choice. They would have to leave. At least now, those living here can choose to stay if they want to, and this beautiful building can be preserved for generations to come."

"Humph," she said, unfolding her arms. "You make your work sound benevolent."

Lee chuckled. "I'm no benefactor. I'm a businessman with some hard facts that the tenants may not have had." He stepped towards her and placed his hand on her back. "Lets go sit down and finish our sodas."

Marisa returned to her stool.

Lee sat next to her. "Did you ever think about how dangerous this building is without a sprinkler system?"

She was taken aback by his question. "I never thought about it, but, now that you mention it, you're right. We have no sprinkler system."

"Nor any smoke detectors, except those battery operated ones that people may or may not have placed in their units. I bet a lot of your neighbors don't even have any type of smoke alarm."

He was making some valid points.

"You know about the rodent problem we had. Rodents carry disease. The leaks the building had before we sealed them up did quite a lot of damage. In some units, we'll have to replace structural posts due to the damage done." Lee sipped his soda and shook his head. "Marisa, this building is a disaster waiting to happen. Without the renovation, it would be only a matter of time before a fire broke out or part of the structure collapsed."

"I had no idea," Marisa said softly.

"Even if the tenants could be allowed to stay on as renters after the renovation, there is no way their rent could stay as low as it is. Nor should they be allowed to pay the same rent they paid for a unit in a dilapidated building when they will be living in an essentially brand new apartment. You understand that, don't you?"

She nodded thoughtfully.

He placed his hand on her shoulder and squeezed her gently. The connection sent waves of warmth through her whole body just as his touch had done to her in the elevator. She had felt the same rush of delight when she held his arm as she helped him after he was hurt outside her apartment. Even working together in the bedroom of this apartment had left her with a feeling of intimacy she had sensed during their confinement on the first day they met.

"Marisa, are you all right?"

She chased away her fanciful thoughts. "Yes, I'm fine. I appreciate your explanation about the building. It gives me new insight into this situation."

"I'm glad I could help."

She looked at him puzzled and wondered if he did indeed like to be helpful. "Randi told me you were helping her to buy her apartment."

He jerked his head at her statement. "She told you that?" He sipped his soda. "I should have told her to keep it under her hat. It was supposed to be just between her and me."

She gave him a wry smirk. "Afraid the world will find out you can be a nice guy if you want to be?"

He grinned at her. "No. I just don't like people talking about my private business deals."

"But Randi is my friend. She tells me just about everything. We've gotten each other through some rough times."

"She seems like a wonderful woman. I like her a lot, but she should have kept our business between us."

"Maybe she broke some cardinal business rule of yours, but she's great. And very talented when it comes to fixing things. I wish I had her skills. I'm totally inexperienced in home improvement, except for that closet I painted," she said.

"And now you know how to remove plaster."

"Right." She sipped her soda. "One thing I can do besides teach is wait tables. I worked as a waitress while I earned my way through college. Starting this week, I'm going to work all day Saturdays and Sundays at Pat O'Reiley's Mexican Restaurant. I'd work during the week, but I have classes I need to take to keep my education up to date for my teaching job. Anyway, I'm hoping I can earn enough to make a down payment on my apartment. I guess I'll know more about that when we get our notices as to how much our units will cost, right?"

"That's true." His face took on an unpleasant, unsure look. "Marisa, I hate to dash your hopes, but I don't think working weekends waitressing is going to earn you enough money over the summer to make a large enough down payment on your apartment. I'm sorry, but, if you want to keep your mortgage payments as low as your rent, you're going to need a sizable down payment."

"Don't say that! Getting that job at Pat O'Reily's is my last hope. I've lost so much. I can't lose another home. I don't want to move away from Randi. She's my best friend."

Lee's jaw became tense. "Marisa, I'm trying to be up front with you. Are you sure you can't work a few more days a week to accumulate your down payment?"

She shook her head. "Pat will only hire people who can work full shifts. He has all the part-time shifts covered. Saturdays and Sundays are the only days I can work more than three or four hours at a time."

"But, if you had the opportunity, you could put in another, say, twenty or thirty hours a week if you could do it in shifts of three or four hours or less?"

"I could, but Pat won't hire me for partial shifts."

Lee studied her for a while before he spoke again. "Would you be interested in a sweat equity program like I'm offering Randi?"

"What?" she asked, stunned at his words.

He took a deep breath and let it out slowly. "I know you don't have the qualifications Randi has, but you showed me a little while ago that you are a fast learner. If Randi, as your old friend, or I, as your new friend, showed you how to do some of the renovations on your apartment, would you be interested in doing them?"

"Yes!" She didn't have to mull over his suggestion more than a half second to know she would do anything to keep her home.

"You're sure?" His eyes suddenly looked as though he regretted making her the offer, like he may have made it expecting her to turn him down.

If that's what he thought, he was wrong. "I'm very sure."

He nodded. "Then we'll see what we can work out. We'll find out what you're capable of doing in your inexperienced capacity and make our deal."

Marisa could still see regret in his eyes. She didn't want to give him a chance to withdraw his offer. She took one more long sip of soda and slid off her stool. "I'd better get home and have a shower. I feel a little grungy from our work."

Lee stood up and took a step toward Marisa. He touched her shoulder. "Will you keep our agreement between us? I don't want everyone in the building asking to be in on the sweat equity program like you and Randi. Too many inexperienced workers would slow us down terribly. Time is money, Marisa. Believe me, I can't afford to come in late on this job."

Was that real worry she saw in his eyes? What were a few dollars one way or the other to a man as rich as L. C. Ramon? "If you prefer I keep our agreement private, I will."

"Thanks, Marisa," he said, letting go of her shoulder.

She turned to walk away, but he took hold of her again and pulled her towards him.

"Marisa . . ." he said softly, his eyes sending her a message she didn't think she should be seeing in him.

"Yes?"

He stared down at her, his gaze seeking the deepest regions of her soul. "I enjoyed working with you."

She could swear he wanted to say something else to her, something intimate and warm, too friendly an exchange for a man and a woman who had only recently met. Worse yet, she wished he would say something more intimate and personal. "I had fun too." Her response was just as devoid of the personal things she wanted to say as his comment was.

He reached toward her and cupped her cheek. This time, he didn't have to say a word. She knew exactly what he was conveying. He had feelings for her that went beyond mere friendship, feelings that should not exist between them, feelings that made no sense in any reasonable world.

Before either of them said with words what their eyes spoke so vividly, Marisa pulled away. "I'll see you in a day or two, Lee." She spun around and left the room before he could stop her, before she could stop herself.

* * *

Lee felt a piece of him leave with Marisa when she walked out the door. He stared after her for a moment, then he slapped his hand on the counter next to him.

"Blast it!" he shouted. What was she doing to him? He was making terrible decisions and offering things he should never have offered, all because of the way he felt when he was around Marisa.

When he was with her, he became a different man, but he didn't understand why. She looked like an ordinary woman, though she was prettier than most. She acted like other women, though she was feistier than some.

He shook his head as if the motion would help to dislodge the confusion in his befuddled brain.

Offering a sweat equity program to Marisa was one of the stupidest things he had ever done. The woman had no experience. What would she actually be able to do to renovate her apartment?

With Randi he had an experienced worker. It made sense to offer her a sweat equity contract, even if such an offer carried a risk for him. Besides, she reminded him too much of Stock's widow. She'd been through the same kind of loss. He owed her. As a widow of a fellow construction worker, she deserved an opportunity.

But he didn't owe Marisa a thing. He'd only known her a little more than a week. Yet, if she had a problem, he wanted to solve it. It mattered to him what she thought, especially about him. She had a way of making him feel better just by entering a room. He liked that feeling, and he needed it more than he would ever admit.

Lee gathered up the soda cans. He emptied the remaining soda into the sink then tossed the cans into the recycle bin.

As he put things in order in the room for the night, he

came across Hal's hard hat. He couldn't help but grin. Hal would find out about Marisa and Randi working for sweat equity. He wouldn't like it at all, but there wouldn't be a thing he could do about it.

Lee chuckled at the thought of his foreman's imminent irritation. He decided even if the sweat equity offers did cost him a little money because of delays in work completion, it would be worth it just to aggravate Hal.

Marisa thought about Lee's offer of sweat equity to help her to purchase her apartment over the next two days. She had received the notice Lee had told her the tenants would be receiving. He had been right about the money she could earn on weekends not being enough for a down payment on her condo. In order to have any hope of staying on in her home, she would have to accept Lee's equity offer.

She had checked with a couple of banks and a mortgage company regarding a home loan. She would need every cent she could earn working at O'Reiley's and a good deal more, which she hoped she could earn through sweat equity, if she wanted to keep her mortgage payments close to what her current rent payments were.

Marisa decided she had better find Lee and lock him into a deal that would give her what she wanted. As she climbed the stairs to the fifth floor, she began to wonder why Lee had made her an offer of sweat equity. With Randi, he obviously made the offer because she was a qualified construction worker. But Marisa had no remodeling skills whatsoever. Offering sweat equity to her made no good business sense at all. And Lee seemed very much the type of man who put business first.

She knew there was something more than business or

friendship going on between them. She wasn't sure what, but there was definitely an attraction, at least physically, if not more. Did Lee have ulterior motives for making her such a generous offer?

Marisa stopped in the middle of the flight of stairs between the fourth and fifth floors. When he had touched her cheek the last time they were together, he had looked at her as though he had wanted to kiss her. What if his kind offer was an attempt at some sort of seduction?

Her cheeks burned at the thought of Lee trying to lure her into an intimate situation. She blushed when she realized she might just enjoy such an interlude.

"Stop it!" she said, scolding herself. Lee didn't have ulterior motives. He merely succumbed to a moment of weakness, and she was not going to let him renege on his offer.

Marisa lifted her chin, straightened her spine and continued up the stairs. This was business. Lee had made an offer, and it was in her best interest to accept it. That's exactly what she was going to do. Then she would have to work her fingers to the bone to learn all she needed to know in order to earn as much equity in her home as possible.

Solid with determination, Marisa turned the corner at the top of the stairs on the fifth floor and came across Sarafina Alvarez who was stepping off the elevator. Marisa inhaled sharply. "Sarafina! I didn't see you. You startled me."

Sarafina pushed her long fingers through her short, white hair. "No harm done, chica." She laid a warm hand on Marisa's arm. "Would you like to come inside for a moment? I would love to chat with you for a while, but it's too hot out here in the hall. It'll be much cooler in my apartment."

More than anything, Marisa wanted to get to Lee to talk to him, but she couldn't turn down Sarafina's offer. She liked the woman very much, and she knew Sarafina loved company. To refuse the older lady's invitation would hurt the woman's feelings. "If you're sure I won't be intruding, I would love to visit with you for a while."

"Bien," Sarafina said, squeezing the hand that rested on Marisa's arm.

As she followed Sarafina into her apartment, Marisa marveled at how well the older woman took care of herself. Her brown skin was aglow with life, her cobalt eyes twinkled with mischief and her hands were always busy, usually working to help others.

When they were inside, Sarafina put the small bag she was carrying on an end table and motioned toward a chair. "Please, sit down," she said to her guest. The elderly woman seated herself on a burgundy love seat and put her feet up on a matching ottoman.

Marisa made herself comfortable in the overstuffed chair that matched her hostess's love seat.

"Have you met Lee Ramon yet?" Sarafina asked as she picked up a piece of patchwork and began to work on it.

"Lee Ramon?" She'd surprised Marisa with her pointed question. "Yes, I met him about two weeks ago."

"Me too. Isn't he a lovely man?"

Marisa hoped the scowl Sarafina's odd comment brought to her face wasn't too obvious to her companion. "You like L. C. Ramon?" Marisa knew Sarafina didn't have much money. She had lived in the building over twenty years, ever since she had retired from teaching. Lee would probably be the cause of Sarafina losing her home. She shouldn't like him.

"Oh, si, of course, I like him. Muy simpatico, chica. I

invited him over for tea and cookies just after he moved into 5F. You know me, I love people. I have to know all about them. When I asked him what he did, he told me he is a land developer. He said he was the one fixing up the outside of the building, the yard, playground and all. He did a top-notch job, don't you think, Marisa?"

"It's much better."

"You feel this?" Sarafina said, waving her arms around her. "It finally isn't hot in here. All I have to do is set the thermostat, and I have cool air, not too cold, not too hot, not too noisy. It's so much better than the window air conditioner I had. That was so old and worthless. How nice it is to come home to cool air after going out in the heat of the day." She took a deep breath. "You wait until you're ninety or so, Marisa, the heat really starts to get to you."

Marisa couldn't help but chuckle. "Houston is hot to everyone, Sarafina, but you are right about the air conditioning. It is very comfortable."

"Wonderful." Sarafina worked on the quilting she held in her hands. She looked at Marisa over the top of her glasses. "I hope you don't mind if I work while we talk. I have much to do."

"Are you making another quilt to raffle for one of your missions?"

"No, this will be a wall hanging."

"Like that one?" Marisa asked, pointing to the small burgundy, gray and black star quilt behind Sarafina that measured about two and a half by three feet.

"In size yes, in subject no. This will be an Ohio star. I will be making fifteen quilted wall hangings with various types of stars. That's what he ordered."

"Fifteen! My goodness, you'll be busy for months."

"It will be worth the work of every stitch."

"You're going to sell them? For your missions?"

"I'm going to sell them, yes, for my missions, no. I have already made six full-size quilts this year for raffles. Tied, not hand-quilted like this one. Mercy, it takes my old fingers months to hand stitch a full size quilt now." She took a deep breath and smiled proudly. "My tied quilts brought in thousands of dollars for my Central American missions."

"Thousands of dollars? Very impressive, Sarafina. Do you mind if I ask who ordered the wall hangings you're making now?"

"Lee Ramon. He's going to decorate the halls of the building with them when the remodeling is done. Star quilts for the Lone Star state. That was my idea. We made a trade. I give him the quilts, he puts up my down payment and arranges a mortgage with payments the same as my rent. Isn't that wonderful?"

Sweat equity, Marisa thought. "Sarafina, that's wonderful. I was so afraid you would have to move. I'm glad you won't."

"Me too. I've grown fond of this place. Oh, I know it's old and run-down, but I like it. It's home to me. Besides, it won't be old and run-down for long. Soon it will be new and beautiful." She took a few stitches, then pulled her glasses off and looked at Marisa thoughtfully. "You know, I shouldn't say it, but all my life I wanted to own a little piece of property. I could never do it, though. Every time I saved for a down payment, one of my missions would be in dire need. There would go my nest egg." She sighed and smiled simultaneously. "My missions are my children. I would give and have always given them everything I can. Nothing brings me more pleasure. Maybe I'm being a little selfish making this deal with Lee Ramon just so I can own a piece of God's earth before I go home to Him, but, in the end, I'll leave my property to the mission. I hope they can be patient." She lifted her chin and looked squarely at Marisa. "Do you think I'm being selfish, chica?"

"From what I know about Lee's plans for the building, I'd say you're making a good investment for your missions. You'll have a fine gift to leave them when you're gone."

"That's what I think too. We both win. I get to realize a dream, and my missions will profit when I'm gone."

Marisa sat forward in her chair. "Sarafina, whose idea was it to use your quilts for the hallway, yours or Lee's?"

The white-haired, brown-skinned woman shifted her cobalt eyes left and right before focusing on Marisa. "You know, I'm not exactly sure how it all came about." Her eyes shifted again. "We were drinking tea and eating cookies, and Mr. Ramon started asking about my quilts. I saw him a few more times, and he asked about my quilts again. Somewhere along the line we discussed the condos and quilts at the same time, buying and selling, you know, business, and all of a sudden we were talking about an exchange—my quilts for this apartment." She put her glasses back on and picked up her sewing. "What does it matter? I got myself a good deal." She took off her glasses again and smiled. "Maybe I shouldn't have taken advantage of the boy." She sat forward and narrowed her gaze. "I know how to make a deal, Marisa. I've had many more years of practice than Mr. Ramon. Why, he couldn't be more than thirty-four or thirty-five years old."

"I don't think you need to worry about Lee Ramon, Sarafina. He can take care of himself."

Sarafina grinned at Marisa. "He has to take care of

himself, chica. He has no wife." She lifted her chin and widened her grin. "While we women do fine without husbands, every man needs a woman in his life. Don't you think?"

"I wouldn't know about that."

"Then you take the wise words of an older woman to heart, chica. I think the man is interested in someone, but I don't know who." She sat back and put her glasses on again. "You know how I like to keep up on things. You let me know if you find anything out about Mr. Ramon and a woman." She started to quilt again. "That man needs someone to look out for him."

Chapter Six

Marisa stood at Lee's door, hesitating before she knocked, thinking about what Sarafina said about Lee needing a woman in his life. Miss Alvarez was a sweet old lady, but she had set Marisa's equilibrium out of kilter with talk of Lee Ramon's love life. The elderly woman had actually got Marisa to wondering if Lee did indeed have a love interest. The thought of Lee being interested in another woman churned her stomach.

She put a hand over her mid section. She was attracted to Lee. She was pretty sure he was attracted to her, but maybe she was wrong. If Sarafina was right . . . Marisa ran her fingers through her hair and tried to chase romantic thoughts of Lee out of her head. She had decided to keep things between them strictly business. That's exactly what she was going to do.

She raised her fist and knocked on Lee's door.

A few moments later, he answered her call. "Hello, Marisa. Won't you come in?"

She stepped inside his efficiency apartment. In an instant, she felt like she was in a private world, a manly, strong world, full of masculine secrets, thoughts and ideas. Lee's world. A world she wanted to know and be a part of. A familiar uneasiness settled over her. "I've just come from Sarafina's," she said, shifting from one foot to the other as she tried to feel comfortable.

"Did you have a nice visit with her?"

"I had an interesting visit with her."

"She's a fascinating woman, isn't she?"

"Very."

"Did you know she was a schoolteacher, like you?"

"You give me too much credit, Lee. Sarafina's reputation as an educator is far better than lowly teachers like myself. She taught various grades in elementary schools for more than fifty years."

"And she started in a one-room, country school in West Texas."

"She's told me some very funny stories about rural schools. Ana Garcia, the woman who lives next door to me, is a children's writer. She's taken many of Sarafina's experiences and turned them into books. One of them she had published."

"Sarafina's biography would make engaging reading, or, better yet, a great movie."

Marisa scrunched up her face. "Just how often do you visit Sarafina? You seem to know an awful lot about her."

A grin inched its way across Lee's face. "Are you jealous, Marisa?"

She eyed him carefully as she folded her arms across her chest. "We're getting off the subject," she said, releasing an exasperated breath.

"I didn't know we had a subject yet. We've been discussing Sarafina since you came in."

"She's the subject."

"You came over to express your admiration for Miss Alvarez? She certainly has mine." He rubbed his fingers over his jaw. "She told me she never married because she never found a man who could keep up with her."

Marisa laughed. "I believe it. Even now as she nears her century mark, she keeps busy with community activities. Up until she was seventy years old she spent her summers teaching in Central America, Guatemala, Honduras and El Salvador, I think."

"El Salvador? That's where my father is from. He went back there after my mother died. He's working with his cousin on his farm."

"You must miss him."

"Very much. I keep trying to talk him into coming back to the States. He wants to come, but he hasn't been able to convince his cousin to move here. He won't leave Marco alone. They're very close."

Marisa nodded and looked away. Then she focused on Lee again. "Did I take you away from some important work?" she asked, waving her hand towards Lee's drawing board.

He glanced at the table, then back at her. "Not really. I was reviewing some plans for the hallways. I don't intend to make too many changes there physically, but I would like to do some cosmetic things and some general decorating. I want the halls to have a nice, homey feel."

"Is that why you ordered fifteen quilts from Sarafina?" she asked, lifting one corner of her mouth.

"She told you about that?"

"She did." She took a step closer to Lee as she unfolded her arms. She lifted her chin and grasped her hands behind her back. "That was a very nice thing to do, taking quilts in exchange for her down payment and manageable mortgage payments."

"Nice has nothing to do with it. I made a business arrangement with Sarafina. Period."

"You didn't know that Sarafina had wanted all her life to own a home of her own?"

He shrugged casually. "Now that you mention it, she may have brought that up during our negotiations."

"Negotiations?" Marisa asked, lifting an eye-brow.

"I do allow for negotiations in business, Marisa. I don't go in like a tyrant and make demands. I make an offer, and, if he or she wants, the buyer or seller makes a counteroffer."

Marisa folded her arms in front of her and bit the corner of her mouth as she studied him, trying to figure him out. "Why did you order all those quilts from Sarafina, really?"

Lee folded his arms as Marisa had done. "If I want a homey effect in the hallways, can you think of anything more efficient at achieving that effect than handmade quilts? Nothing says cozy better than authentic quilts. Sarafina had a product I needed very much. It was purely a business deal."

"And the fact that you were making her dream come true by giving her a chance to own her own home had nothing to do with your purchase of her quilts?"

"It did for her. I had something she wanted, home ownership."

"And she had something you wanted, quilts."

"All business deals work that way, Marisa. Each party has something the other wants." He dropped his arms and stuffed his hands into his pockets. "Let me tell you, that little lady is one tough negotiator. All I wanted was one quilt for each end of the hall on every floor, ten quilts. In exchange I was to give her a break on her down payment. Before I knew what hit me, I was buying fifteen quilts and increasing her down payment so much her mortgage payments will actually be lower than her rent is now."

Marisa chuckled. "Good for her."

"Sure," he chided good-naturedly, "take her side. I've got five more quilts than I wanted, and I'm out a good deal more money than I should be."

"Don't you want fifteen of Sarafina's quilts?"

"Are you kidding? They're works of art. Despite what I said, I know I got a steal." He sidled close to Marisa. "But don't tell her that."

"It'll be our little secret," she said, smiling at him.

Lee stared down at her a moment before he took a step back. "Did you have something else to talk to me about, Marisa?"

"Actually, when I met Sarafina in the hallway, I was on my way to see you to settle our deal for my earning sweat equity to put towards the down payment on my apartment. But talking with Sarafina gave me another idea as well."

"Uh, oh. Don't tell me you have quilts to quilts to sell too."

She grinned and shook her head. "I'm lucky if I can sew an open seam shut again. What I wanted to discuss is this sweat equity program you've offered Randi and me."

"I've got a contract for you right here," he said, turning to a table and retrieving a single piece of paper. "It's a straightforward deal, Marisa. Nothing fancy. Look it over and sign it if you want to go through with it."

Marisa put the paper in her pocket. "I'm sure it's fine, Lee. I'll read it later. Right now there is another matter I want to discuss with you,the idea I came up with while talking to Sarafina." She inhaled and drew on her courage to present her somewhat radical plan. "Your arrangement with Sarafina is a sort of sweat equity since you're trading equity for her quilts, isn't it?"

Lee rubbed his chin with his fingers thoughtfully. "Technically, no, but I suppose a person could look at it that way."

"That's how I see it."

"Okay. I'll concur with you then for argument's sake."

"Good because, in that case, I have a proposition to make."

Lee gave her a tentative look.

"Suppose I could come up with unusual but useful contributions the tenants can make for sweat equity, things like Sarafina's making quilts for the hallway. I think if you are open and flexible to useful but 'thinking outside of the box' contributions to the renovation of the building, we may be able to find a way for just about everyone to gain sweat equity in order to be able to buy their apartments like Randi and I are doing."

His face darkened. "Oh, Marisa," he said, shaking his head, "I don't think so."

"Why not?"

"You're the one with the pet peeves for the wrong use of words, Marisa. Sweat equity means working on one's own property to improve its value. The deal I'm making with you and Randi is straight and legitimate. The deal I made with Sarafina isn't technically sweat equity. It's a special case. We did the deal the way we did because she wanted it that way. She didn't want to move. I wanted her quilts. She preferred an exchange of quilts for a down payment to my outright giving her cash. If she had cash in her hand, she was afraid she'd send it to a mission instead of using it for the down payment. I merely did as she asked." He shook his head. "There's one thing you've got to understand. I'm on a time limit to complete these projects. The more inexperienced people I have involved in the renovation, the bigger risk I run of not completing the projects on time. That could cost me a great deal of money."

Marisa inhaled deeply and blew out her breath. She looked around the room as she thought. "Won't you even consider letting the others earn sweat equity the way Randi and I are going to do?" she asked, looking up at him. "Won't you get to know the tenants' talents a little better to see if you can offer a deal to some of them like you did with Sarafina?"

Lee bit his lip and looked away from her. When his gaze met hers again, his eyes began to soften. "What can I say? I've got a job to do, Marisa, investors to keep happy. I've got responsibilities to a good many people."

"Including the tenants of this building," she said firmly.

He stared down at her for a long moment, obviously thinking over what she had said. He shook his head. "I don't think I can do what you ask."

She narrowed her focus on him and furrowed her brows. She placed her hand on his forearm. "I don't understand, Lee. Why will you help me, Randi and Sarafina but not the others?"

He looked at the fingers grasping his arm. "I can't help everyone, Marisa, only those I think will give me my money's worth. I told you I'm trying to run a business. I've got to watch my bottom line."

She pulled her hand back and nodded slowly. "I see." She took a deep breath, turning away from him and walked to the door. Just before she opened it, she turned back to him. "I'm sorry for bothering you again about the other tenants. I am grateful for what you're doing for Randi, Sarafina and me. I won't let you down. I'm sure Randi and Sarafina won't either." She opened the door and turned to leave.

Lee was behind her in an instant. He shut the door before she could go through, leaving his hand high above her, encasing her between himself and the closed door. He stared down at her for a moment. "Why do you care so much?"

She could barely think with him so close to her. She looked up at him, unsure of how to reply to his very blunt question.

"Why do you worry about whether or not the other tenants will stay or go? It's none of your affair, Marisa. It's their business."

She swallowed hard and tried to pretend he wasn't only inches away from her, staring down at her with his compelling, dark eyes, touching her insides with his gaze. "One of the things I like best about living in this building, Lee, is the neighbors. We have a real community here. We help each other. We watch out for each other. We care about each other." She swallowed over the lump in her throat. "Do you know what I mean?"

He moved his head slowly from side to side. "No, I don't. I've never lived anywhere like that. I've never known a community of people like you describe."

Before she realized her hand had left her side, she found her palm touching his cheek. "I'm so sorry to hear that, Lee, because living in a community like this is very reassuring to a person, especially when times are hard. And here, times are hard more often than they are not."

He placed his hand over the one she held against his cheek. He took her hand into his and kissed her fingers.

"I've never known anyone like you, Marisa." The hand he had been resting above her came down to her face. "You're so beautiful, so caring." As he held her cheek in his palm, he caressed her lower lip with his thumb. He stared at her another moment, then he moved toward her.

When his lips touched hers, Marisa felt her knees weaken. She reached out to him and clung to him to steady herself.

He let go of her hand and wrapped his arm around her waist. The feather light kiss he had given her became deeper.

Marisa moved closer to him. She pressed her palms into his back.

She had been kissed many times before, but Marisa had never been so moved by any kiss as she was by Lee's.

She could live the rest of her life firmly protected inside his arms, kissing him the way he was kissing her now.

He pulled back and took her face into his hands. "I didn't plan for this to happen," he whispered.

She blinked and bit her lip. "I know. If I had known we'd end up like this . . ."

He smiled at her. "Yeah, me too." He let go of her and stepped back. "I suppose you'd better go." He opened the door for her.

"Yes, I better." She stepped through the door, gingerly moving on shaky legs.

"Marisa?"

"Yes?"

"About the sweat equity program . . . bring me any ideas you come up with for the other tenants. I'll see what I can do."

"Really?" she asked, stunned by his change of heart.

He nodded gently. "I won't make any promises, but I will see what I can do."

She stepped toward him and stretched up to kiss his cheek. "Thanks, Lee."

"Don't thank me yet. I may not be able to help your friends, but I will give any suggestions you bring my full consideration."

She pulled her contract from her pocket and raised it in the air. "I'll look this over and get back to you, Lee." When she whirled around to head for the stairs, she nearly ran into Hal Bristo.

He stepped aside and let her pass him. Then he moved toward Lee. "What's going on here, Ramon? I saw what was written at the top of that paper that little lady was going to look over and get back to you about. I know about your deal with Jarvis." He tugged his belt over his belly. "Those two women can't do our work for us, and you know it. Ain't either one of them union."

"Come inside, Hal. We'll talk things over." Lee wasn't going to make the same mistake he had made before with Hal, disturbing the tenants while they spoke in the hall.

Hal stepped inside Lee's apartment without any argument.

Lee closed the door. "Can I get you a cup of coffee?"

The big man took off his hard hat and chased his thick, brown curls with his stubby fingers. "Coffee would be nice. It's been one of those days. Then I find out about this business of you involving two women in our work, and, well, Lee, you just can't do it. You know that. They aren't union."

Lee poured two cups of coffee while Hal talked. Then he gave one cup to his foreman and kept the other for himself.

"Hal," Lee said flatly, "you're the foreman here. I'm the general contractor and the owner of this building."

"But you ain't the only owner, Lee."

He hated being reminded that he'd needed help to take on this project. "Nevertheless, I am the owner, not you. I'm the general contractor, not you."

"You're talking like what I heard is true. You did make a deal with that Jarvis woman to earn equity in her unit? And that teacher, it looked like an equity contract she was waving around just before I come in here. Did you contract with those two non-union women to work on this renovation project?"

Lee sipped his coffee and eyed his foreman carefully. "Yes and no. They will be working only in their own apartments. So, yes, I did contract for them to work in that capacity, though neither of them has yet signed the agreements. Since they will work only in their own homes, which they will buy, they have every right to work without being members of any construction union. So, no, I didn't hire them to work on the renovation project as a whole the way I hired you and the rest of your crew. And I am certainly not breaking any rules or contracts by allowing these tenants to earn equity in their own homes by helping with the renovations in their condos."

Hal took a drink of coffee. He inhaled deeply and let his breath out slowly. "As to whether or not you're breaking any rules, we'll see about that. At the very least, Ramon, you've made a mistake. Letting those amateurs work in their apartments will slow us all down." He took another sip of coffee and shrugged. "As for me, it'll be a burr under my saddle to have to contend with them. But for you, it's going to cost you. They'll slow things down, and you'll lose money on this project like you done on your last job. You lose money again, and won't nobody back you anymore. You'll be lucky to get a bank to finance you a duplex to remodel."

Lee set his coffee aside and folded his arms. "That's my business."

Hal finished the last of his coffee and slammed his cup down on an end table. "Blast it, Ramon, it ain't right. They're not union. They'll slow us down and get in the way. What's the matter with you? You like being a loser?"

Lee sprang forward and nearly grabbed Hal by the collar as he had done before. He stopped himself before he touched his foreman and settled back into a controlled stance. He folded his arms again. "Unless you've got something else to say, Bristo, get out."

Hal put his hard hat back on his head. "I do have one more thing, Lee. I'm warning you right now that you had better not let this equity program of yours go any further than those two women. There will be trouble like you've never seen if it does."

"Are you threatening me?" he asked, stretching to his full height, firming his jaw. "I don't like threats, Bristo."

"I take it from the look in your eyes that you'd fire me right now if you could. But you can't. I came along with Sam Levine's money. I'm part of the package, me and my crew. You're stuck with me." His smirk told Lee he enjoyed his own little bit of power. "If you get yourself any deeper with this equity program you've started, and, I'm sure others are going to want in on it once they hear about it, you'll ruin yourself. I doubt I'd have to lift a finger to make matters worse for you." He widened the smirk on his face. "I won't have to, but that doesn't mean I won't." Hal spun around and walked toward the door. "Thanks for the coffee, Ramon," he said when he turned back as he

Fran Shaff

opened the door. "I've got to admit, it's about the worst I've tasted." He grinned at his own insult and left the room.

Lee picked up his coffee and finished it off. Hal was right about the poison brew just like he was right about almost everything else he said. The tenants could slow the renovation. They could slow it enough to cost lots of money. Lee was sure he could keep Marisa and Randi on track, even if he had to work in their apartments himself to do so. But he'd promised Marisa that he'd consider allowing other tenants to have the same deal he had given Randi and her.

He looked at the cup in his hand and considered throwing it against the wall. He was angry with himself for weakening under Marisa's influence and opening the door to major problems with the other tenants.

Why did he invest in an occupied building? He hadn't anticipated any of the problems he was being faced with. He should have stuck with renovating abandoned buildings.

But this location was so good. The building had so much potential. He had expected to reap a good profit, enough to get him back into investing on his own as he had done all along before.

Things were getting way too complicated. He had let his emotions interfere with good business judgment.

No more. If Marisa brought him a proposal that involved any more tenants working for sweat equity, he would look her suggestions over then promptly and politely reject them.

Hal was right. Amateurs would slow them down, and Lee would bear the brunt of any losses. He was the general contractor for the project. He had to stay on track. His career depended on it. Even if putting business first meant hurting Marisa.

Chapter Seven

As soon as Lee told Marisa he would look at any proposal she brought him for the other tenants, she began to
contact her neighbors about the sweat equity program.

Sometimes she didn't find people at home. When she
received no reply to her knock at the door, she slipped an
envelope into the apartment with a note explaining how
sweat equity worked and asking if the tenant would be
interested in the program to help them purchase their
apartments.

Megan Forest, Lucy Fairbanks and Marcia Toscana,
who were all students and workers of various sorts, had
no interest in purchasing their homes. They all said they
would move to other buildings.

Marisa thought a sweat equity program and the chance
at home ownership would be just what Roger Winslow
needed. He was a troubled man in his fifties, floundering
in life, changing jobs frequently. Roger had joined the
marines at a very young age with an eye toward serving in
the Vietnam war. After his discharge, he had a very unset-

tled life. Even now, decades after the war, Roger was still deeply troubled by his past. Marisa's heart had gone out to him ever since she had come across him sitting alone on the steps outside his apartment when he told her his sad story. She was sure the prospect of working toward a goal like a home of his own would give Roger something positive in his life.

But when Marisa told him rather enthusiastically about the program she was trying to organize, Roger had simply shrugged and said no thanks.

Butch Cromwell, the rather reclusive night watchman, Glen Moore, who was unemployed, auto mechanic Ivan Perkins and Sally Danfield, a dance instructor, all said they would prefer to leave rather than stay.

Molly Winn, a thirty-eight-year-old department store worker wasn't sure what she wanted to do. She told Marisa she would think about the sweat equity program. She did have some interest in it.

Tia Conlin, a hairdresser, and Kenna Luxboro and Tamara Patch, who were both preschool teachers and room-mates were very enthused about the prospect of sweat equity and home ownership. They volunteered to participate in any and all phases of construction as had Melanie Simpson, the telephone operator next door to Marisa, and Jorge Garcia, the minister who lived on the other side of Marisa in 3-D. Jorge's wife, Ana Garcia, a writer of children's books, wanted to help in any way she could. But since she was blind, Ana believed she would get in the way if she was involved in actual construction activities, so she said she could cook for the others while they worked. Then they wouldn't have to take time out to fix themselves something to eat.

Marisa's experiences with the tenants brought her a

mixture of feelings of accomplishment and disappointment. More people had wanted to leave the building than she had thought. Yet she was excited that so many tenants were enthusiastic about working to improve and eventually own their apartments. The sense of community that existed among the tenants who wanted to stay lifted Marisa's spirits and fueled her enthusiasm.

Marisa put off talking to the elderly tenants until last. She feared they couldn't afford their apartments, and she didn't see any way they could work to help defray the costs of their down payments. They just didn't seem physically able.

It had been several days since Marisa had last talked with Lee. She couldn't delay speaking with the remaining tenants any longer. Lee and his crew had finished with the conversion of 3-E and 3-F. The air conditioning was up and running in the apartments and work had begun in the basement on the community room. Lee's crew would begin working on another apartment or two very soon. She had to get her proposals to him before it was too late to work things out with the tenants. She couldn't expect him to wait forever. After all, as he had pointed out many times, he was a businessman, and time is money.

Marisa had four tenants to see who were in their sixties, seventies and eighties. She went to see Harry Baxter in 1-B first.

"Mr. Baxter?" Marisa greeted him with a big smile when he opened the door. "I hope you're doing well today."

Baxter invited her in. During the course of their conversation in which one topic discussed was sweat equity, Marisa learned Baxter had been a bookkeeper for fifty-two years.

"I'm afraid my old body won't let me do things like

painting or plastering anymore," Harry said, swiping his fingers through his white hair, and pushing his glasses up his nose, "but I can still keep records quite accurately. My mind hasn't worn the way my body has."

Marisa admired his eagerness, but she was sure Lee had all the accountants and bookkeepers he needed. "I don't think Mr. Ramon is looking for anyone to do his books, Mr. Baxter."

Harry waved a hand through the air. "Oh, no, of course not," he said, rubbing his stubby fingers over the shadow of beard on his tanned, wrinkled face. "A rich man like Mr. Ramon has a staff of accountants keeping track of his businesses. But for a job like you're talking about, with all those people working at once to do the renovation, Ramon will need a time keeper, someone to keep track of just how many hours of work each individual puts in." He pushed his glasses up his nose again. "What are we talking about so far, maybe a dozen people?"

"I'm hoping to have that many or more by the time I'm finished talking to all the tenants."

"That's a lot of record keeping. Ramon's accountants aren't going to come down here and sit twenty-four hours a day watching people work, and people will be working at all hours, you know. They'll be fitting in time whenever they can."

"You're right. Lee will need someone to keep track of everyone and everything they do." Marisa reflected on Harry's proposal. Then she focused on Harry. "This job might be too big for you to handle yourself, Mr. Baxter. Can you think of anyone else in the building who might help with the time keeping?"

A big smile stretched the wrinkles etched on Harry's tanned face. "Cecelia Escobar headed the nursing department at one of the hospitals in Dallas, or was it Austin, before she retired and moved to Houston. I know a woman in that position keeps meticulous records." He lowered his voice as though he suspected someone might overhear if he didn't. "Don't tell Cecelia this, but I think she may not be so sharp anymore as she was when she was only sixty or seventy years old. However, I can check all her records and make sure they're accurate. She and I have volunteered at the library together many times. She does alright for the most part with her record keeping. I know I can catch any mistakes if she makes them. I'll set up the program for the time keeping so it is foolproof."

Marisa clasped her hands together and smiled a smile as wide as the Rio Grande. "This is wonderful! I'm so happy you've shown me a way that you can participate in the sweat equity program, provided we can get Lee to go along with it."

Harry narrowed his focus on her. "Frankly, when I got the notice about the building going condo, I planned to move. I really didn't want to own property anymore, even if I could afford it, which, as it turns out, I think I could manage even without your equity plan." He rubbed his jaw thoughtfully. "But this sweat equity idea is just the challenge I need. I've been moping and depressed since I lost my Sylvia a year and a half ago. I wanted to go back to work after she died, but no one will hire a man in his seventies. The possibility of working again makes me feel young and vital. When I see Ramon, I'm going to give him my heart-felt thanks."

Marisa put her hands up in front of her. "That might be a bit premature, Mr. Baxter. I still need to write up proposals for the sweat equity program and get Lee to accept them."

Harry waved a hand about nonchalantly. "You'll do fine, and I'm going to thank Ramon just the same. I can't tell you what it means to me to work again."

Marisa smiled at the old gent. Bless his enthusiasm, she thought. "I'd better be going, Mr. Baxter. I'll talk to Cecelia and the others whom I haven't yet chatted with. I'll let you know how things are going."

Harry walked Marisa to the door. "Thanks, Marisa. I look forward to hearing all the details as they're worked out. I can't wait to work again." He shook her hand. "This job means everything to me."

Marisa bade Harry farewell and went home. She grabbed a quick bite to eat before she went to see the rest of the tenants. She talked to Cecelia first. Cecelia said she had every intention of buying her apartment. She liked her home, and nothing or no one could get her to move. When Marisa told her about Harry's proposal, she was as delighted as Harry and for the same reason. Cecelia had worked from the time she was ten years old. She still volunteered at the library, but the idea of having a real job again pleased her more than Marisa imagined it could. And Cecelia promised she'd keep an eye on Harry since he wasn't as sharp as he used to be.

Hazel and Clarence Westfall, retired farmers in their sixties, said they intended to buy their two-bedroom apartment or, hopefully, one of the new three-bedroom units. They wanted to have room for their children and grandchildren to stay when they visited. They didn't need the sweat equity, but they wanted to be a part of the community project. They offered to help Ana Garcia with the food preparations. They would see to it that everyone had plenty of coffee and soft drinks. They also offered to help with clean up.

Tony Atkins, a quiet young man with a reputation for being very helpful to everyone in the building, was reluctant to either commit to or reject the sweat equity idea. Marisa hoped that when Tony made up his mind, he would stay.

The last tenant Marisa was able to reach that day was Ruben Cortez. He greeted her with a total lack of enthusiasm when he opened his door.

"What do you want, Miss Orlando?"

Marisa summoned up a sweet smile. "I've asked you many times before, Ruben, to please call me Marisa."

"Okay. What do you want, Marisa?"

"May I come in? What I have to say won't take long."

Cortez backed up his wheelchair and grudgingly let her into his home. He motioned toward the sofa. "Sit down, if you want. Olivia isn't home right now. She's hardly been home at all the last three months since she started working at that hospital."

"I'm sorry if I've come at an inconvenient time."

"There is no convenient time when you're stuck in a wheelchair Marisa. Six months ago that careless hit and run driver saddled me with this contraption," he said, pounding his wheelchair, "and I won't ever get out of it. He took my wife out of my home. Thirty-four years we've been married, and I could always count on Olivia to be home to take care of me and our kids. Because I can't work, she had to get a job. Now my boy Mano is off who knows where, and I'm all by myself." He took a deep breath. "At least Mano has that Tony Atkins for a friend. He's got someone who can take him places now that I'm laid up."

Marisa wanted to run out of Ruben's apartment. She'd never seen anyone so bitter or anyone with so much right to be bitter. "Maybe I should leave, Ruben."

"You don't have to leave. You caught me grumpy as a wet cat. That's all." He wheeled to a table near the arch between the living room and the kitchen. He picked up a wrinkled paper. "I got your note, the one you left under my door when I was at my doctor's office. At first I wadded it up and threw it in the garbage. What could a man in a wheelchair do, I asked myself? The answer I found surprised me."

"Tell me what you think."

"I worked road construction since I was sixteen. Obviously, I can't do that type of work anymore, but I don't have to be helpless, no matter how much I've been feeling sorry for myself these last six months." He wheeled himself next to the sofa. "Olivia and I have six kids besides Mano. Did you know that, Marisa?"

"Yes. I met most of them after your accident when they came to visit you."

He nodded and went on. "They're all grown now and living in California. Mano's all we got left at home. Anyway, my point is that we used to have a fair-sized home. I did a lot of work in it. Most of the improvements I made in my home I couldn't do from the seat of a chair, but some I could. Painting, for example. All I need is a roller and a long pole. My boy Mano can tape woodwork, ceilings, whatever, so I don't get paint on them, and I can paint ceilings and walls all over the building. I'd be very pleased to work for Mr. Ramon."

Marisa hesitated, not wanting to squelch his enthusiasm. "Ruben, I'm afraid you might be getting the wrong idea," she explained. "Lee isn't exactly going to be hiring anyone to work for him. The idea is that each tenant works in his own apartment and exchanges the value of his or her work for a lower down payment or no down payment or whatever the parties decide is equitable."

He nodded vigorously. "I understand that. What I'm saying is that I can paint. Someone else can rip out walls, another person can plaster. I can trade off with other tenants, painting for plastering, painting for laying carpet, painting for tearing out lathe. Like that. Don't you think Mr. Ramon will go for that?"

Marisa's eyes widened. "I hadn't thought about that." She clapped her hands together. "You've given me an idea Ruben, a very good idea."

"Good," he said, slapping the arms of his chair. "You know I sold my house to give my kids a down payment on a ski resort in California. They all work at the place. They'll show a profit soon, but for now we're all pretty much broke. After I had my accident, the kids wanted Olivia, Mano and me to come out to California, but Houston is our home. I don't want to move." He leaned forward, pushing his elbows into the arms of his chair. "But I sure wouldn't mind owning a piece of God's earth again, even if it isn't on the ground floor. Maybe we could even get one of those three-bedroom units Ramon is making."

Marisa went to Ruben and took his hand into both of hers. "I hope you can, Ruben." She let go of him and pointed herself toward the door. "If you don't mind, I'm going home right now and write up our proposals for Mr. Ramon. The sooner I get the written propositions to him, the sooner we can all get started on our projects." She grabbed his hand once more and shook it again. "Thanks, Ruben. You've just put the icing on the cake."

"I did what?" he called as she raced to the door.

She turned back to him before she stepped into the hallway. "I'll explain later."

Marisa left the Cortez apartment and bolted up the stairs from the second floor to her apartment at 3-C. She spent the rest of the day and half the night writing Lee's proposals. Just before four in the morning, she went to Lee's apartment and shoved an envelope full of hope for her neighbors under his door.

Lee was in the basement working on the community room when he heard Marisa's sweet voice calling him over the noise of a trio of busy hammers. He turned toward her as she walked up to him.

Her face was as bright as the sun, her step lively, her eyes shining and proud. The beautiful sight of her made his stomach do a nervous flip. She wouldn't be happy for long. In a few moments, he'd wipe the smile off her face, turn her steps to lead and dull the shine in her eyes.

He had seen her proposals. He had thought over her suggestions, but there was no way he could give her what she wanted.

How could he let her down? He would rather crush his own heart than break hers.

"Hello, Lee," she said, sending him the loveliest smile he had ever seen.

"Hi, Marisa."

"Forgive me for being so direct, but I just have to know. Did you look at the proposals I left under your door? I worked on them half the night."

Her enthusiasm was killing him. The fact that she had lost sleep in addition to putting so much effort into her work didn't help him feel any better about what he had to do.

He took hold of her arm. "Let's go somewhere a little

quieter to talk." He steered her away from the workman into a bright corner where sunshine poured through three small basement windows.

"I was exhausted when I completed the proposals, but I couldn't sleep much. I was so excited about helping some of the tenants become home owners." She reached out and squeezed his arm. "You wouldn't believe how excited they are, Lee. They're just as happy as Randi and I are."

He shifted from foot to foot and glanced down at the floor before he looked at her squarely. "Marisa, I do appreciate all of your hard work, and I was quite impressed with your creative ideas, especially the time keeper idea and the volunteers who want to help feed everyone while they worked. I was truly touched with the giving efforts the tenants are willing to put forth to help each other."

She beamed with delight. "I just knew you would want to give everyone a chance."

He looked away briefly, then faced her squarely. "I'm sorry, Marisa. I have to reject your proposal."

"What?" Her smile turned to shock. "You don't mean that."

"I'm afraid I do."

"But why?" she asked, shaking her head.

He took a deep breath. "First of all, as I've explained before, the essence of the sweat equity program is for the owners to do the renovating work themselves. Ruben, the man in the wheelchair, can't do anything but paint, according to what you wrote. I'll admit that the Reverend may be capable of remodeling his apartment, but how can his blind wife help? I wouldn't want her to get hurt trying. As for the elderly, we don't need time keepers. We can't use them. We won't be keeping track of anyone's hours, only the progress they are making. Just as in your contract, each person will be required to complete certain steps in remodeling their apartment by certain dates. That is the deal for sweat equity, clear and simple."

"But why can't you bend, make adjustments? Sure, some of the tenants are physically challenged or aged, but they want to work. All they want is a chance."

"And I would give them an opportunity if I could, but I can't. You'll see when you get into taking your apartment apart and putting it back together, Marisa, that this is hard work. We can't have anyone holding us back. We're on a deadline. Time is money, and this project must be completed on time."

"Money is a cold friend, Lee."

"It's the essence of business, Marisa. Without profits, buildings like this don't get renovated, they tumble down with age and waste away. If you like, you can let the other tenants look at your contract. I'll consider offering them the same agreement if any of them are interested. That's the best I can do."

She folded her arms and looked at him with disdain. "I feel sorry for you, L. C. Ramon. You've got an opportunity to do something wonderful for some great people. You could help a strong community become stronger, make a positive difference in people's lives, make some loyal friends. I wish you could have seen the looks on the faces of Harry and Cecelia when they learned they would have a chance at a real job again. If you'd have seen the pride on Ruben's face when he realized he could be useful working from a wheelchair that he felt had taken away his dignity, you'd have felt a sense of satisfaction like you've never known." She took a deep breath and dropped her arms to her sides. "Go take comfort in your bottom line. Warm up with Ben Franklin, Thomas

Jefferson and Alexander Hamilton. And know that your quest for profits will put some very nice people out of their homes." She spun away and stalked off.

Lee wanted to run after her, but once he caught her, what would he say? He had made the only decision he could.

"I'm glad to see you've finally come to your senses."

Lee spun around to face Hal Bristo. "What are you talking about?"

"I couldn't help but overhear. I was working over there," he said, pointing toward a stack of lumber a few feet away. "I guess you took what I said about the amateurs delaying us to heart." He slapped Lee's shoulder. "You'll be glad you listened to me, Ramon, and so will your wallet."

Hearing his own words and attitude reflected in Hal Bristo made Lee very uncomfortable. "How can you be so sure of yourself? Maybe helping these people out a little is something we owe them. They were here before we were."

Hal adjusted his hard hat. "Lee, come on. These aren't the first people you ever displaced. They won't be the last. You've done lots of renovations on buildings all over."

"On abandoned buildings. I've never evicted anyone in my life."

"No kidding?" he asked, scratching the two-days growth along his chin.

"No kidding," Lee said flatly.

Hal slapped his boss's shoulder once more. "It's no big deal. There are plenty of apartments in Houston. One is just like another. Renters know their homes are temporary. If they wanted something more permanent, they would buy their homes."

"That's what I thought when I got involved in this project." Hal was practically quoting him again, and it made Lee more uncomfortable than ever.

"Then you had the right idea. Stick with it. You can't afford to get soft and make offers to handicapped people who can't do a job or old folks who can barely dust a floor let alone paint a wall, lay a carpet or put up sheetrock. Those two women you dragged into this will have a tough enough time, and they're both young and strong."

The more Hal talked, the more Lee felt ashamed of his actions.

The foreman slapped his boss's shoulder one more time. "Stay focused on the project." He stepped back and folded his arms. "One more thing, if that little redhead brings you anyone else who wants a contract like you gave her, turn it down. I heard you get weak with her in the last of your conversation and offer another chance to the able bodied, and I don't blame you. She's a cute little number, but, if she does try to get anyone else in on the deal you offered her, put a stop to it. These two will be enough to reckon with. They'll cost us enough in delays. Don't make matters worse." Hal backed away. "I've got to run out to the truck for my recip saw. Stop by later. I've got a few questions for you on that laundry room job."

Lee nodded. "Sure thing, Bristo. I'll see you in a couple of hours."

Hal turned and walked towards the stairs.

Lee stared after his foreman thinking about what the burly man had just said. In a business sense, he couldn't be more on target. So why did Lee feel so ashamed of himself?

He mulled things over in his mind, reflected on his own attitudes coming out of Hal's mouth and wondered why he now cared whether or not he would displace people with this renovation.

Lee shook his head. "It doesn't matter," he whispered. He didn't need to understand why he felt so ashamed. The fact that he found shame in not giving people every possible chance to retain their homes was enough to make him change his direction.

Besides, maybe Hal was wrong. Maybe amateurs, as his foreman liked to refer to the tenants, would work as efficiently as professionals. Certainly they would be highly motivated if they were working on their own homes.

Lee looked around at the basement under construction. He reflected on the beauty of the newly-completed, three-bedroom apartment he had made from a two-bedroom and an efficiency unit. He loved making homes for people. It was what he had chosen to do with his life.

What would it hurt to take Marisa's words to heart and give the tenants a real chance? At worst, he would lose a little money. He had done that before. At best, the tenants would prove Hal wrong, and he would make a little more money on a project completed ahead of schedule. Lee smiled. He wouldn't mind seeing an opinionated man like Hal proved wrong. But making a little more money wouldn't really be the best that could happen. Right now, the only thing that really mattered to Lee was eliminating his own feelings of shame.

He knew too well what it felt like to have to move from one apartment to another. As a child, he was always moving with his family. His father hadn't been able to speak English very well, and he had a hard time holding down a job. They would sometimes be unable to pay their rent. A few times they were homeless. He knew the heartache of losing a home when he didn't want to move.

Lee made up his mind. He was calling a meeting of the tenants. He would explain the renovations that were going on and offer all of them the same deal he had given Marisa and Randi. That was the best he could do from a business standpoint. It was what he had to do to be able to live with himself.

Once his mind was made up, Lee vowed to never buy another occupied building again.

Chapter Eight

Marisa's week had been an exhausting one. She had started her summer class, talked to the tenants about the sweat equity program, written her proposals for Lee and started her job at Pat O'Reiley's Mexican Restaurant. She had been so busy, she hadn't even had a chance to read over the contract Lee had given her. The one he had given her the day he kissed her.

Her cheeks burned at the memory of his hungry lips teasing and enticing her. Marisa wiped the cool back of her hand over her hot face. She couldn't think about Lee now.

She looked at her watch. One hour remained on her shift at O'Reiley's. Business was beginning to pick up. Time would pass quickly.

As her workday came to a close, the last thing she needed was to see Lee Ramon sitting at a table in her station.

He saw her before she could back away and get another waitress to cover for her. "Hello, Marisa."

"Hi, Lee." She handed him a menu. "Do you want some time to decide what you would like to order?"

He smiled at her. "What would you recommend?"

"If you're in the mood for tacos," she said, "Pat has out-done himself with his pizza tacos. We've sold a ton of them today."

He raised his. "Pizza tacos? Hmm. I like the idea of combining two great foods into one." He handed her his menu. "I'll take an order of pizza tacos."

She wrote his request on a sales ticket. "Anything else?"

"Yes," he said, leaning forward in his booth. "What time do you get off work?"

She cleared her throat. "My shift is over in ten minutes."

"Great. Bring me the tacos and a margarita. I would love it if you would join me for a drink or for something to eat, if you don't have other plans." He sent her another irresistible smile, full of warmth with his sensuous lips and his brown eyes.

"I suppose I could," she said as reluctantly as she could manage. She didn't want to encourage him, but she couldn't make herself turn him down.

He stared at her a moment then said, "I was hoping for a little more enthusiasm."

"Sorry," she said, shrugging. "It's been a long day." She took a deep breath and blew it out. "I should probably just go home," she said, looking away from him. She paused and glanced at him once more. "Besides, we shouldn't be friends, Lee. We're too different."

His lips twisted into a half grin. "I'm not inviting you to Las Vegas for the weekend, Marisa. I'm just asking you to have a margarita and some tacos with me." He softened his features into a full, warm smile. "I like you. I would like to get to know you a little better. As for being different, haven't you ever heard that opposites attract?"

She stared into his glinting brown eyes. "They do?" She shook her head to break the spell he seemed to be settling over her. "I'm tired and hungry. It's been a long day."

"Then sit with me a while and have something to eat."

Even if she wanted to refuse him, she wouldn't have had the strength. She didn't care anymore if they had been at odds the last time they saw each other. She wanted to spend some time with Lee. She liked him. She had been attracted to him ever since they met. What harm could come from sharing a friendly dinner with him? "I'll be back with our meals in a few minutes."

He inclined his head towards her. "I look forward to it."

Marisa hurried to the kitchen. She gave Pat Lee's order and told him to double it. She had been staring at those pizza tacos all day.

Dinner went off amiably. Lee had kept the conversation light. The food and drinks relaxed them. By the time they started to walk home, Marisa was feeling completely comfortable with Lee. She was so at ease with him, she didn't pull away when he took her hand to lead her through a crowd of people waiting to enter a movie theater near the restaurant.

When Lee walked Marisa to her apartment, she leaned into the molding around the door and stared up at him. She felt as though a gentleman was returning her from an arranged date, despite the fact that her hair was disheveled from working all day, and her blouse and shorts were stained with tomato sauce.

Lee raised his hand and placed it on the molding above Marisa's head. He touched her cheek and stroked her hair. "I had a nice time, Marisa. Thanks for having dinner with me."

She smiled up at him. "I'm glad you invited me."

"Could I take you to O'Reiley's another time, for a real date, one where I call you up," he said, toying with a strand of hair that had fallen from her braid, "and you say, 'Why, Lee, I would love to go out with you,' and I say, 'Great, I'll pick you up Monday after the meeting'? You did agree to go with me to O'Reiley's before, remember?"

When he stood this close to her, looking at her with provocative dark eyes, she had a hard time remembering anything. If he leaned a little lower, took possession of her lips, she would promise him whatever he wanted.

"I remember," she finally admitted. *Easy, Marisa.* She reminded herself she didn't really want to encourage Lee's interest in her. She could never get seriously involved with a man who placed money at the top of his priority list the way he did. "But that was before, Lee."

"And this is now, Marisa. I knew the first day I met you I wanted to get to know you better. Now I'm more sure than ever that we need to spend some time together. We owe it to ourselves, especially after . . ." He caressed her cheek and stroked her lips with his thumb. ". . . after the moment we shared in my apartment a few days ago."

She could feel her cheeks turning as red as her hair.

He was leaning so close to her, tempting her, making her want him to kiss her again. "Is it a date? Monday night after the meeting?"

She started to shake her head, then she stopped. "What meeting?"

"The tenants' meeting."

"What tenants' meeting?"

"Didn't you get the envelope I slid under the door last night?"

She thought a moment. "The envelope, of course, I

found it this morning as I was going to work, but I didn't have time to read what was inside." She took a breath and brushed a stray strand of hair from her face. "You've called a meeting for the tenants?"

"Yes, Monday night. I want to explain to everyone in the building what the renovation will entail, what they can expect to see in the way of changes, and I want to offer them the same deal I've given you and Randi for sweat equity."

"But what about those who aren't able bodied enough to work like Randi and I can? Can you offer them something like you offered Sarafina?"

"Marisa," he said, stroking her cheek with the back of his fingers, "we'll talk about that on Monday at the meeting. Right now I want to know if you'll have dinner with me after the meeting at O'Reiley's or anywhere else you say?"

Her heart told her to grab onto his invitation and savor it until they could be together again eating, drinking and laughing as they'd done a few moments earlier. But her head warned her not to trust him. She hadn't figured him out yet. When the meeting was over, maybe she would understand him better, depending on how he handled the needs of the tenants. "Ask me again Monday when the meeting is over. I'll let you know then."

He took a step back and shoved his hands into the pockets of his khaki pants. "You're not an easy woman to please," he said, grinning at her.

She smiled at him, took out her keys and unlocked her door. She gave him one last look before she went into her apartment. "You'd do well to remember that, Mr. Ramon."

Marisa arrived in 3-E to find Lee talking with Harry Baxter as other tenants of the building chatted casually.

She held the sweat equity contract Lee had given her in her hand. She still hadn't read it, thanks to another busy day at the restaurant on Sunday and a full day of classes on Monday.

Most of the tenants who had stated an intention to stay on in the building were already in 3-E when Marisa arrived. She took her seat in one of the white wooden folding chairs Lee had set up in the living room for the meeting. Tony and Molly, who had both been unsure about buying their condos, were at the meeting too. Marisa was glad they had decided to join the rest of the group.

Lee was wearing a polo shirt and khaki pants, his usual attire when he wasn't in his working jeans and light blue shirt. Today's polo shirt was a dark brown. Marisa admired the way the rich color set off Lee's wheat-colored skin, molasses hair and deep brown eyes. Today he appeared more handsome than ever.

Her heart skipped a beat. She had laid awake most nights ever since she had met Lee Ramon wondering how she could be so magnetically attracted to a man who placed the value of money ahead of the needs of people. Maybe he wasn't as devoid of compassion as she thought. She would know more after the meeting was over.

Marisa glanced at Lee, and he smiled at her. Her heart stopped for a full three seconds. She returned his smile without meaning to, and he winked at her.

She shut her eyes tightly. She couldn't allow her heart to move any closer to Lee's, not until she understood him better.

Lee's deep, commanding voice rang over the noise of the group in the room. "Everyone, we're ready to start the meeting."

People who were standing, sat down. Everyone turned toward Lee. A hush fell over the room.

"First of all, I want to thank all of you for coming today. I hope each of you had a chance to look around this apartment before the meeting so you can see how we intend to finish the other units in the building."

Most of the heads in the group began to bob up and down.

"You've done a beautiful job, son," Sarafina said above the slight noise of the people gathered. "If the other units turn out as nice as this one, we're going to have some very fine homes when this is all done."

Sarafina had barely finished her comment when someone in the group began to applaud. The others followed with approving enthusiasm. Marisa was surprised to find herself joining the crowd. Lee had indeed done a top-notch job converting 3-E and 3-F into a lovely new three-bedroom apartment, now known as 3-E. His work was perfect right down to the oak trim and hardwood floors. The rooms were all nice sizes and perfectly arranged. He had made the best use of his limited square footage, giving the future owners of the unit the most value for their dollar.

When the group quieted down again, Lee continued. "I hope all of you have read over my asking prices for the renovated condos you're living in now. I also hope that all of you have read over the contracts I included regarding the sweat equity I'm offering to help you buy your apartments. I would like to say to all of you who might be planning to take advantage of the opportunity to gain equity in your apartments, that we are going to have to have one hundred percent cooperation from you. My crew and I are on a deadline to complete this renovation. We can't

have anyone holding us back. I want to be clear on that."
He paused and looked around the room before he went
on. "Before we get into the details of the contracts, let me
tell you a little about what my aspirations are for this
building."

His smile showed a great sense of pride. "My goal for
this building is to create a clean, welcome, homey envi-
ronment for families, singles, elderly and young, free of
any of the previous infestations of rodents or the damage
from leaks or improper maintenance."

Applause interrupted him along with a couple of
whistles.

Marisa stared at Lee as a smile lit his face again. He
looked as though he were blushing. Did the appreciative
applause actually embarrass this bold man?

The room quieted. "You may have noticed over there,"
Lee said, pointing, "behind those folding doors off the
end of the kitchen work area, near the large linen closet, is
a washer and dryer. Each unit will have its own washer
and dryer which will—"

Thunderous applause and more whistles interrupted
Lee. He put his hands up in an effort to quiet the people in
the room, but they insisted on showing appreciation a
while longer before they finally gave in to Lee's request
for silence.

"Which will eliminate the need for a community laundry room in the basement. The former laundry room will
be converted to more storage units for the various apartments as well as a kitchen to accompany the community
room."

Someone started to applaud again, but Lee stopped
them by raising his hands and saying two words. "Please,
don't."

A giggle rumbled through the room, and Lee went on. "Each of you who are going to sign a sales agreement to buy your apartment will be able to make requests as to how you would like your unit finished. In some cases we will be able to enlarge rooms or make them smaller, depending on the need for the walls in the support of the building. We'll also be able to build in more storage, book shelves, whirlpool tubs, showers that help with special needs, things like that. Of course, these amenities will cost extra money for the unit. Contact me to see the plans for the condo you want to purchase. If you want any changes, tell me as soon as possible. All changes will have to be made before we can sign purchase agreements. Purchase agreements will be drawn up in the next few days. They should be signed as soon as possible. I want them all back within seventy-two hours of receipt. Any agreement not signed and returned by then, will be withdrawn. Sales prices for units are not guaranteed and are subject to change, so make sure you sign the purchase agreements and get them back to me within the allotted time."

No applause now, Marisa noted. Lee had finished his glorification of the building's improvements and was moving on to the dollars and cents facts of the tenants' homes.

"I want all of you to understand completely and thoroughly just how this sweat equity program is to work." Lee's gaze stiffened as his eyes moved to rest momentarily on every single person in the room. When his focus fell on Marisa, she felt a shiver travel up her spine. "The amount of equity you earn is up to you. You make arrangements with me before you sign the contract. You must complete whatever home improvement jobs you agree to do no later than the time allotted for the work to be done. Anyone who does not complete the renovation projects named in his or her contract by the date the projects are due to be completed will lose all equity the individual has earned to that point. This equity will be treated like earnest money, which is forfeited when a sale is not completed. Those tenants losing this sweat equity may renegotiate a sale for their unit if they are still interested in buying it, but they must then pay cash or secure other financing. There will be no further opportunity to participate in another sweat equity program." His stern gaze drifted over the crowd again. "Anyone who backs out on the sale also loses accumulated equity credit as they would lose earnest money."

Marisa felt a knot in her stomach. Lee's rules were hard, devoid of compassion. Dear heaven, did he have a plan to make it impossible for the tenants to keep their agreements so he could have a building full of renovated apartments remodeled with free labor? Did her own contract read as harsh as Lee's words sounded? She opened her envelope and looked at the contract for the first time. When she finished reading it, she dropped her hands in her lap. She should have read the agreement before she got the other tenants involved. She was more afraid for her neighbors than ever. Lee was a severe man when it came to business. He made sure his bottom line wasn't a broken line. The tenants could work hard for weeks and end up with nothing to show for it if they missed one of the deadlines.

"Any questions?" Lee asked.

"Yes," Ruben Cortez stated in his commanding voice. "So you can fix my shower in such a way that I can actually get in there and bathe like I used to before I ended up in this contraption?" He slapped the arms of his wheel chair as he spoke.

"Absolutely, Ruben. In fact, with the renovation, we will be complying with all rules and guidelines of the American Disabilities Act, or ADA, as it's called. This will make the entire building more accessible to people restricted to wheel chairs like yourself, people who have difficulty getting around in general and to the blind as well. Door handles will be easier to use, all signs will be in Braille and so on. Speaking of signs, they will be written in both English and Spanish since so many of us in Texas speak either or both languages. And please," Lee said, moving his eyes over the crowd again, "if any of you have any other suggestions of how we can make the building more accessible to the residents, give me your ideas."

Cecelia raised her hand.

"Yes?" Lee replied.

"If it wouldn't be too much trouble, Lee, could we have some security at the front door. I would feel much safer if people couldn't just walk in off the street. You know a few months back and a couple of years before there were some people associated with drugs coming and going in the building." She paused, and the crowd murmured and nodded. "I know I would feel a lot safer if we had a security system."

Lee smiled at Cecelia. "I'm sorry, I forgot to mention in my opening remarks that we will indeed have a security system. When a visitor arrives he'll press a button to call you on your phone. You will then be able to let him in through your current phone system."

Cecelia put a hand to her heart and smiled. "Thanks, Lee."

Lee nodded toward Cecelia. "Any other questions?" he asked, looking around the room.

"I've got another one," Ruben said, his voice sounding a little angry.

"Yes?" Lee replied.

"This contract here," Ruben said, waving the paper Lee had included in the envelopes he had given the tenants, "says we get equity for work done in our own apartments, not anyone else's."

"That's right, Ruben."

"But that's not what I understood. When I spoke to Marisa, we talked about trading off work in each other's apartments. I'm restricted by what I can do nowadays. But I could paint. If someone would help me with my demolition, putting up Sheetrock and so on, I could trade off painting," he said, looking around the room. He looked back at Lee. "How would that work, Lee?"

"I'm afraid that would be up to you tenants individually if you wanted to make this some kind of community project or a trade off of work. As far as I'm concerned, all I care about is that the jobs you contract to do get done to my satisfaction and on the agreed-upon time." He lifted a hand. "Which reminds me, your work will be inspected on a daily basis. Everything has got to be done according to code. If you don't follow explicit instructions, you'll be responsible for getting the job done again until it is done right. If you want to trade work with other tenants, you will be responsible for whatever the other tenant does in your unit. I refer you to the contract agreements."

He looked around the room. "Any other questions?" He waited a moment, then said, "If not, Ana Garcia has provided us with some fresh-baked goodies. Ana told me Hazel Westfall made the punch and her husband cooked up his special coffee recipe. Ana wanted to be sure you didn't hold her responsible for Clarence's coffee if his special brew is a disaster."

The tenants chuckled, and Lee grinned.

"Don't throw cookies at me yet," Clarence said, standing and pulling up the pants that slid down to the thin man's hips. He lifted his skinny chin and chased thick brown curls with his fingers. "Taste the coffee first. You might even like it."

The tenants talked and enjoyed refreshments after the meeting. Marisa tried to get a feel for the reaction of some of the tenants. She heard a few of them making deals to trade work as Ruben had suggested. The younger tenants seemed enthusiastic about the adventure of remodeling their homes, but Marisa wasn't sure if they had a realistic idea about what it took to do the job they were going to sign up to do. The young ladies seemed more preoccupied with the colors they would paint their rooms than the hard work of demolition and reconstruction.

The elderly people spoke of having nieces or nephews help them with their remodeling. None of them really needed the sweat equity if they wanted to buy their apartments, according to what they had told Marisa, but they were excited at having an opportunity to work at a job again, any job, even a laborious one.

Marisa began to worry whether any of the tenants truly understood just how difficult the task of renovation would be. Suppose they took on more than they could handle. Once they failed to complete their contracts as agreed, they would lose their earned equity and their homes. It would be her fault for getting them involved and Lee's for making such harsh demands in his contract.

"Marisa?" Lee said as the last of the tenants drifted out of 3-E.

She jumped. "I didn't hear you, Lee."

"You did look pretty deep in thought. I hope you were thinking about me and our dinner tonight," he said, smiling down at her.

She shook her head. "Not at all." She lifted her chin, squared her shoulders and said, "There will be no dinner for us tonight." She whirled away from him and hastened to leave the room.

He caught her before she could go. He took hold of her shoulder and turned her back to face him. "Marisa, what's wrong? I just gave you what you've been asking for, a chance for your neighbors to stay here in this building. I thought you would be happy."

"You've got to be kidding! You're setting up my neighbors for failure," she said without trying to hide her exasperation.

"I did what? Failure? What are you talking about?"

She jerked away from him. "What difference does it make? You don't understand." She took a step back. "If you want to take advantage of them, go ahead. I can't stop you." She took a deep breath and shook her head. "When you told me on Saturday night after we had such a nice time together that you were going to give the tenants a chance to earn sweat equity so they could buy their homes, I thought you had grown a real heart. I thought you wanted to help."

He folded his arms across his chest. "I do want to help. I am helping. What more could I do?"

"You could ease up. You're being so unreasonable. You said we'll lose our earned equity if we don't meet our deadlines. What if we have trouble of some sort and a certain phase of the project puts us two or three days late? We'll lose all the equity we earned, right?"

He shrugged. "That would depend on the trouble, to an extent. For example, if someone carelessly broke a water pipe and did damage that delayed the renovation, then, yes, I would say that would be the tenant's fault same as it would be a contractor's fault. Damages done on a job are the responsibility of the person who causes the problem, and they make restitution. Now, if a hail storm rains down on us, windows break and delays are caused by something like that, things would be different. Insurance would pay for damages, and tenants would be given a grace period just as a contractor would."

"And if someone gets hurt and can't do their job?"

He unfolded his arms and shoved his hands into his pockets. "That would be like the first example."

She shook her head and glanced toward the door. "I'd better go before I say something I don't want to say." She looked back at him. "I had hoped I was wrong about you, Lee. I had hoped you would have a real heart instead of a cash register beneath your ribs." She took a deep breath. "All that matters to you is your profits." She turned to leave, but he grabbed her arm and made her look at him again.

"You're wrong, Marisa," he said, his eyes blazing down on her. "I care much more than you know about something other than my business."

She went weak under his intense gaze as she wondered if what he meant was that he cared about her. She feared her knees would buckle beneath his power, and she would succumb to his hold over her heart.

"I have a job to do," he said flatly. "I'll do it as I see fit." He let go of her arm and touched her cheek. "But that doesn't mean I won't help wherever I can." He stroked her cheek. "If I can help you in any way, Marisa, you just say the word." He pulled his hand back. "But the contracts are as they are. I won't change a thing in them."

Marisa took a breath to steady herself. "I'm sorry to hear that, Lee."

"I'm sorry to have to say it, but I do have obligations."

"So do we all."

"It wasn't my intention to upset you, Marisa."

She swallowed over the lump in her throat. "I have to go, Lee."

"I understand," he said, folding his arms and stepping back.

She stared at him a moment longer, wishing things were different between them. "Good-bye, Lee." She turned to leave.

"Good-bye, Marisa."

As she walked down the hall to her apartment, Lee's final words reached her heart. His good-bye sounded so permanent. It hurt more than she thought anything could.

Chapter Nine

Marisa leaned against the wall outside Randi's apartment as she left Lee in 3-E. A few minutes later, her friend appeared at the top of the stairs carrying a basket of laundry.

"Hi, Marisa," Randi said. She raised her basket up. "I'm glad I won't have to be making this trek much longer. Cliff dirties more clothes than any six adults. It'll be nice to have washers and dryers in our apartments."

"Yeah," Marisa replied, only half hearing what Randi was saying.

The thin blond eyed her neighbor carefully. "What's wrong?" Randi asked. "You look like you lost your best friend, or your heart has been broken, or both."

Marisa felt herself tearing up. "I feel that way too."

Randi placed her basket on her hip and took hold of Marisa's arm. "You come inside for a while. We'll get to the bottom of this."

Marisa put up no struggle against her dear friend. She needed to talk to someone about her confused feelings, and Randi was the perfect friend. She listened well, spoke empathetically, and she always had good insight. "Thanks. I could use a good talk, if you don't mind."

She took Marisa to her front door and opened it.

The inside of apartment 3-A was a disaster. "You're already remodeling," Marisa said as she watched Randi close the door and place her laundry on the kitchen table in the corner.

"Yup," she said proudly. "You mean you haven't heard all my noise?"

Marisa shrugged. "There are all kinds of construction noises going on all over the building, but I didn't know any of the commotion was coming from you."

"It is, and I'm thrilled." She smiled and lifted her shoulders as she slipped her hands into the pockets of her cutoffs. "I feel alive again, Marisa, and I haven't for so long. I've missed this work. Doing it makes me feel like the person I was before Mac died. I loved working with him, but I loved the work too." She took her hands out of her pockets and motioned to the green plaid sofa that had been shoved into a corner and covered with heavy plastic. "Want to sit down?"

"Sure." Marisa walked to the couch and sat.

Randi yawned as she lowered herself to her seat two cushions away from her neighbor. "One of the side benefits of this kind of work is getting tired enough to sleep a solid eight hours at night." She ran her fingers through her hair and yawned once more. "It's been a long time since I slept through the night. I can't tell you how wonderful it feels to get a good sleep."

"But how can you sleep? Aren't you worried about keeping the mandates of Lee's contract? Don't you realize that if you miss one deadline you'll lose everything?"

Randi slid next to Marisa and took hold of her hand. "Easy, honey. You're talking nonsense. What do you mean I should be worried? You sound as though Lee is trying to cheat us or something. The man is giving us a chance at a dream. Why are you so upset?"

Marisa bolted from the sofa. "Are we talking about the same man? Did we read the same contract?"

"The contract I signed with Lee is the same one he gave to all the tenants, so, yes, we read the same contract. Why? Do you think there's something wrong with the agreement he offered?"

"Yes!" She stuck her hands into her hair and tugged. "There is most definitely something wrong with those contracts. If any of us slips up, Lee gets everything, including apartments renovated with free labor."

"Whoa," Randi said, standing and taking hold of Marisa's arms. "Honey, you've got to calm down. You're talking nonsense."

"I wish I were. You don't know how much I wish Lee Ramon were someone besides a man who saw nothing more in life but ways to profit in business dealings."

"Marisa," Randi said softly as she studied her friend carefully, "you've got a personal interest in Lee, don't you?"

She bit her lip and nodded slowly.

"And he's done something to disillusion you, is that right?"

She lifted her chin. "He's trying to take advantage of the tenants, getting their hopes up, then yanking the rug out from underneath us when we fail to meet a deadline. His contracts are too hard. I don't think I'm even going to sign mine." She took a breath, furrowed her brows and went on. "I told you I talked to the other tenants and made a proposal to Lee where we could all work on each others' units and get equity that way, didn't I?"

Randi nodded.

"Well, Lee threw that idea out the window. We have to do our own work in our own apartments, and we're each responsible for any work done in our units."

"But what's wrong with that? That's what sweat equity means."

Marisa let out an exasperated breath.

Randi led her to the couch. "Sit. We need to get some things straightened out."

Marisa sat where she'd been a few minutes before.

Her hostess sat next to her. "First of all, there isn't a thing wrong with Lee's contracts. The fact that he is offering us sweat equity at all is extremely generous of him. He doesn't have to put up with tenants that may or may not be able to do a job most of us have never done before. He has every legal right to simply end our tenancies at the end of the sixty days notice he gave us, and send us on our ways if we don't have the money to purchase our units." Randi paused. "You understand that, don't you, Marisa?"

"Of course," she said, folding her arms.

"Second of all, Lee's contracts are pretty much standard issue as far as penalties go, though they're a little different from contracts given to contractors because of the nature of their dealing with home owners. All contractors pay some sort of penalty if their projects don't meet standards, are done late or don't stand up to some other provision of a contract. That's just the way business is done."

"Humph," Marisa grunted. "Now you're sounding like Lee."

Randi chuckled. "Thank you. I take that as a compliment since I used to be in the same business, though Mac and I were never as successful as Lee, unfortunately."

Marisa could almost feel her friend's scrutiny as Randi looked at her thoughtfully.

"What do you think Lee should have done that he hasn't done already?"

Marisa shrugged, took a deep breath and laid her head back on the sofa. "I don't know," she said, blowing out her breath. "I'm afraid. That's all I know. I'm so afraid."

Randi squeezed Marisa's shoulder. "What are you afraid of? That you won't be able to go through with buying your apartment? That you might have steered your neighbors wrong by working to get everyone involved in the sweat equity program Lee offered us? That maybe you care a little too much for Lee? That maybe you made him into some kind of white knight, and you found out he's just as human as the rest of us?"

Marisa slowly took in all of Randi's suggestions and began to sort through them. "All of the above." Tears welled up in her eyes.

Randi hugged her then pulled away. "Great. We know what you fear, now we'll eliminate your troubles one by one."

Marisa wiped tears from her cheeks. "Just like that."

"Why not?" She shrugged and put up her hands. "Your problems aren't insurmountable. They aren't even especially difficult. In ten minutes, we'll have them all solved."

"Sure we will," Marisa said, smiling sardonically.

"Don't believe me?" Randi teased. "Okay, I'll prove it to you." She took a deep breath and touched the index finger of one hand to the index finger of the other. "First and foremost, you, like me, want to own your home, right?"

"Absolutely."

"But you're afraid you won't be able to live up to your contract—maybe because your classes or your extra job will interfere, the time you need to devote to your mother might get in the way, whatever your reason."

"Right."

"Those are legitimate fears, Marisa, but nothing will stop you if you make up your mind that you want to buy your apartment. We'll see to that."

"We?" she asked, raising her brows.

"Yes, we. The tenants. We'll all work together just like you proposed to Lee. We'll make our own arrangements like we have done tons of times when one of us has needed help. Remember when Ruben was hurt in his accident? Cecelia got us on schedule to take meals to the Cortezes, run errands for them, drive their son to his school activities and handle everything else they needed help with."

"I love this community, Randi. I don't want to lose it."

"I feel the same way. When Tia broke her leg, we all pitched in then too and took care of her. We got her groceries, took her to doctor appointments and so on. As I remember, Sarafina even found another beautician to take Tia's place temporarily so she wouldn't lose her job or her clients, didn't she?"

"She did," Marisa said as she fondly remembered more of the times the neighbors had worked together to help one another.

"We'll have another meeting ASAP. Tomorrow, if I can arrange it. We'll have it here so people can see what they'll be living with while they're remodeling. They need to know just what they'll be getting into before they sign contracts with Lee. We'll work out a shared work program for those who want to participate like you discussed with the tenants. Lee said at his meeting he would have no objection to such an arrangement. He just didn't want to be directly involved in the plans for it."

"Randi, your enthusiasm is beginning to rub off on me," Marisa said, grinning.

Her friend returned her smile. "Good. Working with other people always makes the job easier, and we can encourage each other. Most importantly, we'll keep each other on time. We won't let any one of us fail. When our apartments are renovated, they will be homes that we own, not just units we rent. They'll be investments in a beautiful new building, Marisa." Randi rubbed her arms. "I get goose bumps just thinking of it. It's going to be wonderful. This building will be a showplace. Lee has excellent vision. We're all going to profit from this adventure."

Randi's excitement filled the room. Her enthusiasm was contagious. Suddenly, Marisa believed everything her friend told her about the success of the renovation, and she began to have confidence that she would one day soon realize a dream. She would own her own home again, and she would retain the neighbors who had grown to mean so much to her. "You make it all seem possible, Randi."

"It is possible, and it will happen. I guarantee it. Now," Randi said, shifting on the sofa, "the next item on the fear list is Lee Ramon."

Marisa felt her cheeks warming. "I don't think you've got anything in your tool box that could help me where my feelings for Lee are concerned."

"You're probably right about that, but I do have something to say about him."

"Do I want to hear it?"

Randi shrugged. "Does it matter?"

Marisa laughed. "I suppose not. You're going to tell me anyway."

"Right. I always say what I think, don't I?"

"Whether I want you to or not."

Randi touched Marisa's hand and smiled. "You know me so well." She pulled her hand back. "Lee is a fine man, Marisa. Did you know he's been taking Cliff to the community center to teach him how to play the piano?"

"He has?"

"Yup, every other day when I get home from work, for a half hour at a time."

"Wow," Marisa said softly.

"Exactly. Despite the fact that you think he's a single-minded businessman who can't see past profits, if you look at him without the blinders of preconceived ideas, you'll find a man with a generous heart." She paused while Marisa took in what she had said. "But you'll have to make your own discoveries, honey. That's the way it is with a man and a woman. It's the way it's always been. I don't think that will ever change." A smile tugged at her lips. "I hope it doesn't."

"I'm not sure . . ."

". . . whether you want to discover anything more about Lee?"

"Yes." Marisa wrinkled her nose. "Does that make sense?"

"Of course. You've had a lot to deal with since your mother's stroke. Her illness, your bills, losing your house and car. Those tough breaks have taken their toll on your emotions. It's only natural you would hesitate to explore another emotional issue in your life. And if you go where your feelings for Lee may lead you, you will experience emotion like you've never known before, Marisa. Believe me. If you choose a road together, it could be a very poignant one." Randi took a deep breath and sighed. "There is nothing in life so wonderful as love."

"It's a road that could lead to disaster."

"Or to happiness like you've never known."

Cliff came barreling into the room. "Mom, my movie is done. I need you to read me my book." He looked at Marisa. "Hi, Marisa."

"Hello, Cliff. What book do you have tonight?"

"Jack Kicks Back."

"Would you mind if I read it to you?"

"That'd be great, if it's okay with Mom."

"I'd appreciate it very much, Marisa," Randi said. "I've got more work I want to get done before the quiet hours begin for the night."

"I love reading to Cliff," Marisa said. She did enjoy spending time with Randi's son, but at the moment she didn't want to go home to an empty apartment. She had always enjoyed her privacy, but, ever since she'd met Lee, she didn't like being alone anymore. She knew it made no sense, but neither did most of the feelings she'd experienced since the day the broken elevator put her and Lee on an altered course for the future. She wondered if life would ever make sense again.

Two days after the meeting Lee held, Randi hosted a meeting of her own. All the tenants who'd attended Lee's gathering came to Randi's. In addition, Roger Winslow, the Vietnam veteran and Harper Bosanko, an unemployed stock broker Marisa hadn't been able to talk to before she made her proposal for Lee, attended the tenants meeting in 3-A.

Randi lit a fire under the group of neighbors and ended up involving everyone at the gathering in the community project except Sarafina Alvarez. Her quilts would keep her too busy to become involved in renovation, but that didn't stop her from wanting to know everything that was going on.

Each tenant decided to commit to a different amount of work. Some wanted no more to do than prime and paint new walls and maybe stain woodwork. Others wanted to be involved in everything from tearing out plaster to hanging Sheetrock and laying flooring.

Tenants set up their work exchanges in the group and made sure either they or their work partners would be able to complete jobs at certain times. Then they invited Lee to join the meeting and okay all the due dates so he could coordinate them with the work he needed his plumbers and electricians to do.

A week into the project, things were running smoothly. An argument would break out between the tenants from time to time on some of the work, but such discourse was quickly put to rest. As agreed at the meeting, Harry Baxter and Cecelia Escobar mediated the disagreements, and tenants abided by whatever the elderly duo decided.

Marisa was wearing herself to a frazzle going to classes, taking care of her mother, working at Pat O'Reiley's and laboring at the renovation project, but, like Randi, she believed the physical strain of the remodeling was worth every ache and pain.

She hadn't seen much of Lee except to pass him in the building. They would exchange a quick greeting, and Marisa would move on, hoping she would not give Lee any chance to invite her out again. Her feelings for him were so unstable. She found herself powerfully attracted to him whenever she saw him or thought of him, but she was afraid to encourage a relationship that could bring her more pain. She had had more than her share of pain in the last two years, and she just wasn't up to taking a risk with Lee.

As Marisa studied one evening, she slammed her book shut and tossed her highlighter pen aside. She had had enough of researching the psychology of the young adolescent. She needed some fresh air.

She slipped into a pair of sneakers, tucked her keys into the pocket of her cutoffs, put on a clean sleeveless green shirt and left her apartment to go for a walk in the park. She decided maybe she would get an ice cream. The evening was hot, as most are in Houston in summer, and an ice cream would be the perfect refreshment on a sultry night.

She strolled down the street, taking note of the other apartment buildings she passed. For the first time, she began to see improvements that should be done on the old neighborhood's deteriorating structures. She wondered if the other buildings had the same kind of wide oak woodwork her apartment had, if they had rodent problems like they used to have or if anyone would be fixing up the neighboring buildings the way Lee, his crew and so many of her neighbors were renovating their building.

A sense of pride began to well inside her. She had been against the renovation from the beginning, fearing she and her neighbors would be displaced. Now, as they all worked together, she was so proud of what was happening in her apartment building. The antique structure would indeed be the jewel of the block when the renovation was completed. More importantly, Marisa would be a home owner once again. That meant everything to her.

As she quickened her pace toward the park, someone stepped next to her.

"May I join you?"

Her heart skipped a beat at the sound of Lee's voice. She looked up at him, pleased that he was at her side at that particular moment when she was feeling so good about the renovation. "Hello, Lee," she said, smiling up at him.

"Are you going somewhere in particular, or are you just taking a walk?"

Marisa took a breath and let out a sigh. "I've been cooped up in my apartment studying the behavior of twelve, thirteen and fourteen year olds all afternoon. I came out to get some air."

"Yikes," Lee said, "sounds like you've been stuck in a bit of a nightmare."

Marisa laughed lightly. "It isn't as bad as it sounds, but I definitely needed to set my studies aside for a while."

"I'm on my way to the park. Harry Baxter told me there's a vendor there that makes the best tacos in town."

"Mr. Rae. Harry's right. He's got great ice cream too. He gets it from a local dairy that makes frozen treats better than any you've ever tasted. I was thinking about visiting Mr. Rae myself."

"Then we're headed in exactly the right direction." Lee took hold of Marisa's arm. "You will join me, won't you?"

She smiled up at him. "That might be nice." So much for her resolve to steer clear of the man she found so attractive. Marisa allowed herself an inward sigh. Sharing an ice cream or a taco with Lee wouldn't hurt a thing. And having some company was just what she needed at the moment.

Lee returned her smile.

Heaven help her weak, wobbly knees. His smile could make her melt, and that just wouldn't do.

Chapter Ten

"I love the outdoors," Marisa said when they reached the park. "I grew up on a farm, you know."

"You did?"

"Yes. A dairy farm, not far from the city."

"A dairy farm, huh? When I think of rural Texas, I always think of ranches, never dairy farms."

"Well there are dairy farms in Texas. Wisconsin doesn't supply milk for the entire country, you know."

"Wisconsin?"

"It's known as the dairy state."

"Oh, that's right. I've been there. When I lived in Chicago. Great cheese, good football team."

"We had a terrific pond on our farm."

"Did it have fish in it?"

"No, but it did have frogs and pollywogs. They were fun to catch and play with."

"What about water moccasins?"

"None of those, thank goodness."

"So you liked playing in the pond, huh?"

"I loved it. My friend Lara and I used to sneak away when I was supposed to be doing chores just to play in the water and catch frogs."

A derisive grin slid over Lee's face. "Want to relive a childhood memory?"

Marisa wasn't sure what he was getting at. "Like what?" she replied suspiciously.

A second later Lee swept her up into his arms. He began walking toward a small body of water, the remnant of a seven-inch down pour from two nights before. He wore a grin the size of Alaska on his face.

Marisa struggled against him. "Lee, put me down. Where are you going? What are you going to do?"

"I'm going to give you back a piece of your childhood."

"No," she said, kicking her feet. "I'm twenty-eight years old. I'm too old to relive my first childhood and too young for a second."

"Nonsense," he replied. "You'll love it."

Marisa continued to gently protest, and Lee proceeded to the rain-filled ravine. When he reached the water's edge, he kept on walking. He waded until he was thigh deep. "Okay, Marisa. Now I'll set you down."

She grabbed him tightly. "No, not now!"

He set her down. "How's that? Feel like a kid again?"

She let go of him and laughed. "Almost." She took a step toward shore and lost her balance and she went down.

Lee reached toward her and gave her a hand.

Marisa came out of the water wiping her face and laughing. "Now I feel like a kid again."

Lee laughed with her and tugged her toward shore. "I didn't mean for you to get completely drenched, Marisa. I'm sorry. I just thought we'd do a little wading. Whenever we get a good drenching like we had the other night, the parks fill with all sorts of water holes. I used to love to play in them when I was a kid. They never last long, but they are always great fun for sloshing around."

"I don't mind getting soaked. The water actually feels kind of good." And being in his arms wasn't bad either.

"I bet," he said, not believing her. "You're a good sport anyway."

When they left the water, Lee took her to a picnic table. She sat while Lee flagged down a boy walking through the park carrying a towel.

"Hey, son, could I buy that towel from you? I'll give you twenty dollars."

The fair-skinned boy with red hair and freckles widened his deep blue eyes. "Twenty bucks for a towel? Sure thing, mister."

Lee pulled a twenty from his wallet and handed it to the boy. "Where were you going with that towel anyway?"

"I'm meeting some friends at the other side of the park. The creek there backed up and flooded a big piece of the picnic area. It's a great place to swim in. That big rain we had did some of the best flooding I've ever seen. The water hole I'm going to is three times the size of the small one over there," he said, pointing to the body of water Lee had walked into with Marisa. "We've got to swim before the water soaks away."

"Then you'd better get going," Lee said. "Have fun swimming, and thanks for the towel."

"You bet, mister. Thanks for the twenty," the boy said as he ran off.

Lee sat next to Marisa. He took the towel and began to dab at her hair and face.

Marisa let him pamper her for a minute, then she took the towel from him. "I'll do it," she said. She finished drying her hair, then she wiped her sleeveless green shirt and her legs. She stood and wrapped the towel around her shorts and sat down again.

"Do you still want something to eat?"

Marisa glanced over to see Mr. Rae and his cart full of sandwiches, tacos, hot dogs and ice cream. "I'd love a chocolate ice cream."

Lee moved close to her on the bench of the picnic table. "And I'd love to get it for you." He reached toward her and trailed his fingers through her wet hair. "You're very beautiful, Marisa."

She stared at him for a long quiet moment, their eyes communicating without any need for words.

Lee moved closer.

She shifted next to him and lifted her face to him. She wanted him to touch her.

His lips were mere millimeters from hers when a child's voice stopped them cold. "Hey, mister," the boy said.

Lee looked at the boy he'd bought the towel from earlier. "My friends want to sell their towels, too."

A group of boys had joined the red-headed moppet, each of them holding up their towels.

"No thanks, boys," Lee said. "I don't need anymore towels." He reached for his wallet. "I'll tell you what, though, let's go over to Mr. Rae's cart. The ice cream is on me."

The boys gave up a joyous holler and dashed toward the vender.

"I'll be back in a few minutes," Lee said to Marisa.

She nodded and watched him walk away. Marisa took a deep breath. She didn't know whether to throttle the boys or thank them. If they hadn't interrupted, Lee would have kissed her. She had wanted him to kiss her, but it may not have been a good idea. No matter how much she was attracted to Lee, she still wasn't sure she could trust him.

When Lee returned with the ice cream, their conversation took a friendly tone and consisted of harmless banter. After they'd eaten, they headed home.

By the time they reached the doorway of Marisa's apartment, she was laughing and having more fun than she'd had in many months.

"Did you forget all about the child psychology you were studying this afternoon?"

"I certainly did." She looked up into Lee's warm, brown eyes. "Thank you for taking me away from my hectic schedule for a while," she said.

He lifted his hand above her and pressed it into the molding around her door. "It was purely my pleasure, Marisa. I'd like to take you out some place a lot nicer than Mr. Rae's next time. How about Friday night? We could go the restaurant at that new hotel. I think it's called *El Cielo de los Estrellas.*"

"That's a long name for a restaurant, but it sounds quite romantic. How would you translate it? Stars of heaven? Stars of the sky? Sky full of stars?"

He touched her hair, her cheek, her chin. "I think any of those translations would do, but you're avoiding giving me an answer. Will you join me at that new romantic restaurant or not?"

She stared up at him, mesmerized by the warmth of his eyes, feeling the heat from his body pierce the air between them and settle against her skin. "Lee, I . . ."

He touched her lips with his fingers. "Don't say no." He lowered his lips to hers and kissed her before she could say another word.

Encased between him and the doorway, she still wasn't close enough to him. Without breaking the bond of their lips she moved closer and slid her hands up his chest until they met at the nape of his neck.

He wrapped her in his arms and kissed her more ardently.

Marisa tried to stop the loving connection their kiss was burning on her soul, but she couldn't. The longer he touched her, held her, kissed her, the more her need for him burned on the spirit inside her.

A door slammed and voices echoed through the stairway from the floor below.

Lee pulled back and looked down at her. "Is that a yes?"

She looked up at him trying to remember what he'd asked her.

"You will go out with me on Friday night?"

"Yes, Lee."

He smiled and kissed her lightly. "Good. I'll see you on Friday night." He kissed her once more, then he left.

As Marisa watched him bound up the stairs toward his apartment, his long legs taking two steps at a time, she knew she'd done the right thing accepting Lee's offer. She had to get to know him better. Whether she trusted him or not, she was in love with him. If she was going to let herself care for him, she had to learn more about him. And she had to learn to trust him.

Lee couldn't believe he'd finally talked Marisa into going out with him. Their evening at *El Cielo de los Estrellas* was the most romantic he'd ever had.

Marisa was more gorgeous than ever in her green and white halter sundress. She wore her hair down, allowing her mass of red curls to flow over her shoulders, tempting him all evening to take the copper strands into his fingers.

It had been nearly impossible to leave her when the evening ended. He needed her next to him. He was beginning to crave her the way he required air when he'd run all five flights of stairs in the apartment building. But he didn't want to hurry her into anything she might not be ready for. It had taken him long enough just to get her to go out to dinner with him.

Lee went through his mail when he arrived home after his date. He read a disturbing letter from his father, tossed it aside and decided to go outside for a while. He had too many things on his mind to be able to get any sleep.

He went to the yard in back of the building. A screened-in gazebo had recently been built. Lee seated himself in the swing inside the pine-scented structure. The thick padding of the swing soothed the aching muscles that came with the intense work he'd done throughout the week.

The sultry evening air washed over Lee, mixing scents of roses from the bushes next door with the pine aromas of new construction. Lee took a deep breath and laid his head back. He closed his eyes and turned his thoughts to his father.

The letter he'd just read said his uncle had had a mild heart attack. It wasn't serious, but it upset Lee just the same. Lee wished he could talk his father into coming back to Texas. He missed him very much. What if it was his father who had the heart attack instead of his uncle?

Lee bolted to his feet and walked to the screen panel opposite the door. He stared at the thick, tall bushes that enclosed the back yard. His dad was fine. His uncle would be fine.

He had enough to worry over without stewing about his father or his uncle. Hal had been riding him about the non-union tenants working in the sweat equity program. He continued to complain about the *amateurs,* and he threatened a lawsuit for breech of contract because Lee was letting non-union people work on the renovations. In addition, his foreman continued to taunt him with talk of losses he believed Lee would suffer on the project. As if he needed Bristo to remind him how fragile his financial condition was.

Lee was only too aware that he could lose everything on this renovation if things didn't go according to plan. That was why he was working fifteen hours a day to help the tenants stay on time with their work while managing the other thousand things that needed doing each day.

Lee took a deep breath and shoved his hands into the pockets of the khaki pants he'd changed into after his date with Marisa.

"Penny for your thoughts."

Lee spun around. "Marisa. I didn't hear you."

She closed the door behind her as she stepped inside the gazebo. "I came out to get some air. I couldn't sleep." She stepped closer to him. "I guess you had the same problem."

He shook his head as he looked down at her through a mixture of moonlight and the yellow illumination from the backyard security lights. "Don't know if I'd have been able to fall asleep or not. I didn't try."

Her emerald eyes looked almost black in the low light. "You seemed fine this evening. Has something happened since you brought me home?"

Lee decided she must not have realized that thoughts of her were enough to give him insomnia. So he went along with her. "I got a letter from my dad. My uncle had a heart attack. He's going to be fine, but—"

"But you're worried anyway," she interjected. "I understand."

He smiled at her. "I guess you do. You know all about worrying about parents." He stepped next to her and withdrew his hands from his pockets. "Would you like to sit down?" he asked, waving a hand toward the swing he'd been sitting in a moment before.

"Yes," Marisa said softly. She moved to the swing and made herself comfortable on the soft cushions.

Lee sat beside her, leaving room between them. He began to move the swing back and forth. "It's awful warm tonight." He laid his head against the high back of the swing.

"I like hot nights. I always have."

Lee looked at her and smiled. "It's a good thing then that you live in Houston."

Marisa returned his smile. "I suppose."

"I'm glad you live in Houston," Lee said. The smile left his face. He stared into Marisa's engaging eyes.

"Me too." Her words came on a raspy voice.

Lee's hand drifted toward Marisa's cheek before he even realized it had left his side. His fingers grazed the rosy roundness of her silken complexion. "You are so beautiful, Marisa."

She blinked as she stared up at him. "Lee, you shouldn't tell me that."

"Why not?"

"It's likely to go to my head," she said, grinning at him.

He moved a little closer. "I don't care. It's the truth. You're absolutely lovely."

Marisa looked away. When she looked back at him, she said. "Maybe I should go inside."

He touched her cheek again. "Do you think you can go to sleep now?"

She stared up at him and slowly moved her head from side to side. "No."

"Neither can I." He moved closer to Marisa and laced his fingers in her hair. Copper silk, just as he'd remembered. She was wearing the dress she'd worn to their dinner, and her hair cascaded over her bare shoulders.

Marisa gazed up at him, then she closed her eyes.

When he brought his lips down on hers, his heart jolted. The kiss they shared held a kind of magic beyond any imagination. Barriers faded. Sultry evening air turned to tropical sweetness. Dreams joined with reality.

Marisa moved closer and snuggled against Lee's chest.

He wrapped his arms around her tightly and intensified the kiss.

Profound was too weak a word to describe the intense feelings provoked by Marisa's kiss. Ecstatic was too mundane a description to characterize the way this union with her made him feel.

Lee suddenly pulled away. He held her face in his hands. "Marisa," he whispered, staring down at her.

She blinked three times revealing deep desire, hiding it, then divulging it again. She had the most beautiful eyes and hair, the softest, honey-colored skin.

He kissed her again. He couldn't have stopped himself even if he wanted to. And he didn't want to. He needed her.

Marisa held him tightly and urged him to move beyond their modest connection.

Lee wanted nothing more than to oblige her, to remain in the world of rapture the two of them had created, to touch her, hold her and cuddle her. He lifted her to his lap and pressed her closer. "Marisa . . ." He kissed her forehead. "Marisa, should we be doing this? Are you ready for this?"

She snuggled closer to him, pressing her cheek against his. "I don't know what is right or wrong anymore, what we should and shouldn't be doing. All I know is that I want to be with you."

He pulled back from her. He stared down at her and pushed her copper locks away from her face. "And I want to be with you."

"Lee," she said, pulling back and looking up at him, "what have you done to me?"

"What have I done to you? What do you mean?"

She stared up at him, her dark eyes glistening in the low light. "You must have done something to me to make me feel this way. I've never felt about any man the way I feel about you, Lee." She slid off his lap and walked to the opposite side of the screened-in structure. "And I shouldn't feel this way." She turned around to face him. "We are nothing alike. I shouldn't be attracted to you."

He smiled, stood and walked over to her. "And why is that? Are there rules I don't know about regarding who a woman can and cannot be attracted to?"

"That's not what I mean. You know what I mean. We look at things differently, important things. If I'm going to care for a man, I have to know who he is. I have to understand him completely, and we've got to have some things in common."

He toyed with the curls resting on her shoulder. "I won't explain myself to you, Marisa. There are some things you have to learn for yourself. Only then will you truly understand me."

She looked down and turned away. She walked to the door and opened it before she looked back at him. "If you don't want to explain yourself, then you will remain a mystery to me, and I will never let this happen again."

Lee went to her. He didn't let her leave. "*This* is no mystery, Marisa." He'd barely said the words when his lips captured hers. He kissed her more thoroughly than he'd ever kissed her before. He wanted to make his feelings for her crystal clear.

She was breathless when he pulled back. "Lee," she said, gasping for air. "Why did you do that?"

A sardonic smile etched itself on his face. "Because I wanted to, and because you wanted me to. How is that for having something in common?" He grasped her shoulders and stared into her verdant eyes. "Don't casually cast off what we have, Marisa. It's far too rare to be taken lightly."

She took a deep breath and stared up at him.

He kissed her softly. "Think about what I said. Think about how you feel right now." He opened the door for her and watched her walk toward the building. "I'll see you in a couple of days," he called.

Lee almost never prayed, but, as Marisa moved farther away from him, he asked God to help her understand how much he loved her. He needed Marisa more than he'd ever needed anyone in his life. Somehow, she had to come to realize that, and she had to make that discovery on her own.

Chapter Eleven

Marisa started her preparations to take her mother to get her hair washed. She asked for assistance in getting her into a wheelchair, took her to the beauty parlor of the nursing home and washed her mother's hair as she'd done for many months.

As a rule, Marisa didn't speak much to Ariane while she took care of her, but on this visit, she couldn't seem to keep still. After being with Lee the previous night, her heart was full, so full her words spilled over her lips telling of the joy and confusion she felt in loving Lee.

Her mother made little response to Marisa's confessions of love and bewilderment. The best the devoted daughter could hope for was that her mother at least felt less lonely hearing about her child's life. Marisa knew it made herself feel better to tell her mother her deepest secrets, even though the woman couldn't respond.

Back in her mother's room, Marisa combed her mother's hair gently. "I wish I knew what to do about Lee.

138

When I think of him, my heart leaps. I'm quite sure I love him, but I'm not at all sure I understand him. I can't move forward as I'm sure he wants to do until I have no doubt he is the kind of man that I want to love."

Marisa paused, waiting for a response from her mother, any response—a blink, a moan, a movement. She neither heard nor saw anything.

She put the comb away and took out a nail file. She started to give Ariane her weekly manicure. "I wonder if I'll ever figure him out, Mama." She looked up from the fingers she was working on straight into her mother's eyes. "I need to understand him."

Her mother moved her fingers ever so slightly. Marisa knew it was probably some sort of involuntary movement, but she treated it as though it were an attempt at communication.

She looked up, stood next to her mother and squeezed her hand. "Did you want something, Mama?"

She made no response.

Marisa squeezed her mother's hand again, then she sat and went back to giving her the manicure. Blast the stroke, Marisa shouted mentally. She wanted her mother back. She needed her mother. There was no one else to tell her what she needed to hear. It was her mother's duty to tell her to stop being such a scared kitten. She wanted to hear her mother tell her to stop hedging where Lee was concerned and just love the man. She'd met him to love him. He'd come into her life and made her feel wonderful things she never knew existed. Her mother should be telling her to grow up and become a woman, a total, complete, one hundred percent woman by totally and completely loving her man.

Marisa smiled at that last thought. Right after her mother made that statement, Marisa would accuse her of being old fashioned, but she'd follow the sage advice nevertheless because it was the right thing to do.

"Mama," Marisa said as she finished her manicure, "thanks for listening to me. If you could speak to me, I think I know what you'd say, and I'm going to take your advice. I'm going to talk to Lee and tell him how I feel." She brushed her hand over her mother's hair and kissed her cheek. "I have to go to work at the restaurant now, Mama. I've got the late shift today and the early shift tomorrow. I'll find Lee after work tomorrow and tell him I love him. I'll tell him I want to take time to get to know him and understand him. He's worth the effort, Mama, and he's worth the risk. I'll tell him that, Mama. It is indeed time I stopped acting like a frightened little girl." She kissed her mother once more and left for Pat O'Reiley's.

Marisa spent two grueling days working at the restaurant, thinking about seeing Lee when she finished her Sunday shift, worrying if she would say or do the right things when she told Lee how she felt about him.

When her shift ended on Sunday, Marisa started home, rehearsing on the way what she wanted to tell Lee.

She went to the elevator to go up to her apartment when she arrived back at her building. Men were working on the lift, making it temporarily unavailable. Strange that workmen were logging golden hours on a Sunday. The elevator must have quit working again. Marisa didn't feel like taking the stairs after such a tiring day, but she didn't have a choice.

When she turned at the landing that led from the second floor to the third, Marisa was nearly hit by a flying duffel bag. She stopped at the open door of apartment 2-F. "Roger, what's going on?"

Roger Winslow, a lanky, shaggy man in his fifties with dark eyes and fuzzy gray hair, came to the door. "That scoundrel who took over the building is throwing me out."

"But why? You signed a contract to buy one of the one-bedroom apartments, didn't you?"

"That's right," he said, setting another bag in the hallway.

Marisa shrugged. "Even if you didn't, you wouldn't have to leave yet, not for at least another month. That's what our initial notices said."

"Doesn't matter what it says on any piece of paper when a man like Lee Ramon wants to line his pockets. You know he's remaking the units that are efficiencies and two-bedrooms next to each other into three-bedroom apartments. Well, the two-bedroom next door to me is vacant now, and Ramon can't wait to get started taking my place apart to make another one of those fancy three-bedroom places. He needs me out."

Marisa's stomach started to churn. "But he has no grounds. He can't just throw you out."

"He thinks he can. You see, I was a week late with my rent." He took a deep breath and rubbed his fingers over his scruffy jaw. "You know how it is sometimes. Sometimes it's hard to get my hands on the rent. That's why I went for this sweat equity thing. I figured I'd be banking money while I work before I even see it. If I had a responsibility like mortgage payments instead of rent, I'd do better. You know how it is."

Marisa knew. Roger had told her all about his life

months before, that he'd been in Vietnam when he was barely eighteen years old, that he had problems because of his experiences, he couldn't hold a job for long, and he liked wine a little more than he should. The poor man had tremendous difficulties resulting from courageous efforts in service to his country. Marisa believed Roger deserved understanding. The fact that he had joined the sweat equity program for the reasons he just stated showed he was trying to take steps in the right direction. "Could I lend you the rent, Roger? Would that help?" She needed the money she was earning at Pat O'Reiley's herself, but she had to help Roger if she could. She wouldn't let down one of her neighbors.

Roger scratched his scruffy face and dragged his fingers through his tangled hair as he shook his head. "Wouldn't do any good. Ramon has his mind made up."

"Maybe I could talk to him." Surely she would have some influence over a man who cared for her as much as she was sure Lee did.

"Thanks, red," he said, fluffing her copper locks with his fingers in a fatherly gesture, "but I don't need your help. I'll find another place." He drew his hand back and shoved it into the pocket of his jeans.

"Good luck, Roger."

"Good-bye, red. Take good care of the kids at school. We all need them, you know."

"I will, Roger." Marisa turned away and went up the stairs to the third floor. Her heart ached. For two days she'd spent the majority of her time imagining the exchange between Lee and her as she told him she was in love with him. But could she really be in love with a man who would callously toss a Vietnam veteran on the street just because he was a week late with his rent?

Lee couldn't be like that, could he? Perhaps there was more to the story than Roger had told her.

Marisa went into her apartment. She showered to clean herself up and cool down. She washed the grime away with no more than usual effort, but she didn't cool down. She was angry, fighting mad livid. How dare Lee treat her friend so harshly? She couldn't wait another minute. She had to see Lee, but not to tell him she loved him. She'd never tell him she loved him. It would be pointless to love a man whom she didn't like, and, right now, she didn't like Lee Ramon at all. Still, she had to try to intercede on Roger's behalf. He'd been her friend for some time. She had to try to help him keep his home.

Marisa went out into the hall and gave herself a moment to collect her thoughts and determine how to approach Lee about Roger. Then she started up the stairs towards the fifth floor to Lee's apartment.

As she reached the landing on the fourth floor, she heard Lee's voice echoing through the halls. It came from the left. He must have started work in 4-A, the only vacant apartment on the fourth floor.

Marisa turned toward the sound of Lee's irate voice. When she reached 4-A she saw Lee scolding one of the crew. It seemed the elevator repairers weren't the only workers logging overtime on a Sunday.

As Lee reprimanded the woman who'd made a mistake in studding a wall, he told her to work from the set of plans next time. He made it clear that she was not to assume that every apartment was to be finished exactly alike.

Marisa turned away. She decided now was not a good time to approach Lee to ask for any favors for Roger. He was in too foul a mood.

Lee saw her before she got away. "Marisa."

She turned to face him.

His whole demeanor changed when he laid eyes on her. His anger disappeared like darkness at the end of a solar eclipse. He went to her and took her hands. He smiled down on her. "Good evening," he said softly.

The second he touched her, she nearly forgot why she'd sought him out. "Hi, Lee."

"How did work go this weekend?"

"Fine," she replied evenly.

"You look wonderful," he said, his eyes scanning her face, green sleeveless blouse and cutoffs.

Lee was in his work clothes, light blue shirt and jeans. Whatever he wore, he was unbelievably handsome. His provocative eyes continued to stare down at her.

Marisa pulled her hands away from him. "Lee, I've got to talk to you."

He slipped his arm around her shoulders and led her out into the hall. "Want to go up to my place and have a cup of coffee?"

"No," she said, moving away from him.

He wrinkled a brow. "Marisa, what's wrong?"

She looked around the hall, then back at Lee. "Can we go into one of the rooms of the apartment? I don't want to be overheard."

"Sure." He placed his hand at the small of her back and guided her into one of the bedrooms of the two-bedroom apartment. Once they were inside, he closed the door.

He leaned against a wall and folded his arms. "What's this all about?"

"I saw Roger Winslow a little while ago. He told me you were throwing him out of the building."

"That's right."

"But why?" She was stunned by his candid response. She'd expected him to say something defensive.

Lee stood up straight and firmed his jaw. "That doesn't concern you, Marisa."

"He told me he was a week late with his rent. I'll pay it, Lee. I'll write you a check right now."

"I won't discuss this with you, Marisa. What happened between Roger and me is business. Ours. Not yours."

"But, Lee, you don't understand Roger. I'm sure if you understood him, you wouldn't make him leave. He's trying to put his life together. That's why he signed to join in the equity program. He's had a hard life, Lee. He needs our compassion and our help."

Lee moved closer to Marisa. He stroked her cheek with the backs of his fingers. "I don't want to talk about Roger, Marisa. I'd rather talk about us."

She closed her eyes when his velvet caress burned her skin. "Lee, don't," she said with no hint of protest in her voice whatsoever.

He grasped her chin and kissed her lightly.

When he pulled back, Marisa looked up at him.

"Something very special is happening between us, Marisa." He took her in his arms and kissed her again. This time his lips lingered on hers for a blissful eternity.

Marisa suddenly cared about nothing but the splendor of Lee's warmth and strength surrounding her, penetrating her to her very core.

When he pulled away again, she tugged him back to her.

Hungry, strong male body clung to her, delighting her beyond anything she'd ever known. Nothing had ever taken her breath the way Lee did.

Lee pulled back, but he didn't let her go. He stared

down at her. "I think you agree with me," he said, smiling down at her.

"Agree with you, Lee? About what?" He seemed to have stolen her common sense as well as her breath.

"That something special is happening between us."

She pushed him away and took two steps back. "I don't understand it, Lee."

He moved to her and took her in his arms again. "What's to understand?" He brushed copper strands from her face with his fingers. "Don't analyze, Marisa. Enjoy it. Let it happen." He leaned down to kiss her again, but she stopped him.

"No," she said, pushing herself away again.

"Now I don't understand," he said, obviously bewildered and confused. "You kiss me like you are losing your heart to me the same way I am losing my heart to you, then you push me away. Have you committed yourself to someone else that I don't know about?"

She shook her head. "There's no one else."

"Then what is the problem? Do I have bad breath? Am I too tall? Do you dislike the color of my hair, my eyes or my skin? Are my arms too long or my neck too short? Why won't you grab what is happening between us and savor it instead of fighting it?"

She whirled away from him and walked to the window. She looked out on the sidewalk forty feet below. The whole world seemed to be coupled up. How she wanted to put everything aside and cling to Lee the way other women clung to their men.

She spun back to face him, arms taut across her chest, her steel chin lifted in the air. "I can't get involved with a man I don't understand."

"We already are involved, Marisa." He stepped toward her, touched her cheek with his finger tips and drew back his hand. "As far as knowing me or understanding me is concerned, look into your heart. You'll find the answer there."

"Sometimes," she said, tears beginning to choke off her voice, "sometimes a woman's heart can lead her in the wrong direction." She lifted her chin higher. "When we're together like we were a moment ago, the way we were two nights ago in the gazebo, everything between us is wonderful. In the elevator when we first met, you were kind and compassionate with me when I was afraid. With Cliff you're generous with your time and your talent for the piano. Friday night you made me feel like . . . like our hearts were joined, as though they beat as one."

He cupped her chin with his hand. "Is that a bad thing?"

"Of course not. It's wonderful." She took a step back. She needed distance if she was to say what she had to say. "Lee, you're another man too." She squeezed her hands into fists and held them in front of her. "It's so infuriating. How can the man who is so gentle and caring with me and so kind and generous with Cliff be so heartless with a troubled veteran like Roger Winslow?"

"But one has nothing to do with the other."

"You see?" Marisa said, opening her fists and swinging her arms around her. "That's what I mean. You don't see how they are related, but I do." She took a deep breath and let it out slowly. "A man who is truly kind, generous and gentle could never throw a person like Roger on the street. He was only a boy when he did a tour of duty with the Marines during the Vietnam war, Lee. He saw things so horrifying that they stole peace from his life. His service to our country cost him his ability to keep a job, to fight his drinking problem, probably even his ability to sleep peacefully at night. We owe him, Lee. He deserves at least our compassion."

Lee folded his arms and bit the corner of his mouth while he stared down at her. Then he said in a purely business tone, "I told you, Marisa, that I will not discuss Roger Winslow with you. His eviction is business pure and simple. It's between him and me. It doesn't concern you."

She narrowed her focus on him and gritted her teeth. "You are heartless." She stormed toward the door. Before she opened it, she looked back at him. "You must be a very good actor, Lee. I believed you could care deeply about people if you wanted to."

He followed her to the door and placed his hand high above her head against the molding. "I do care, Marisa, especially about you."

She put her hands over her ears. "I won't listen to anything more you say." She lowered her hands and lifted her chin. "I'm going home. At least I have a home. Roger doesn't. You've never been homeless, Lee. You don't know what a horrible thing that is or you never would have thrown Roger out."

Lee pulled his hand away from the door and folded his arms. "You're wrong about me, Marisa. Some day you will see that."

"No, I won't see anything of the kind. I don't want anything else to do with you, Lee, except to complete the business deal between us." She grasped the door knob and turned it. "If you want to talk business with me, Lee,

I promise I'll be civil. Otherwise . . ." Tears began to choke her words. "Otherwise leave me alone. I can't be involved with a man who doesn't share my beliefs of being compassionate with the less fortunate." She turned and stormed out of the room.

Lee watched the woman he wanted next to him every minute of the day leave him in a cloud of angry dust. He could have her back in a heartbeat if he'd tell her the truth about Roger Winslow, but he couldn't bring himself to talk about others in a negative way—not even to keep Marisa. He couldn't help it. That's just the way he was.

Hal Bristo came to the bedroom door where Lee was standing. He looked from Lee to the door Marisa had gone through and back at Lee again. "Ticked her off, did you?" He glanced at the door once more, then at Lee. "You got a real knack for riling her."

"She was asking me about Winslow. She's upset that I've thrown him out."

"You didn't explain things to her?"

Lee shook his head. "It's none of her business nor anyone else's."

"I suppose not, but you could have saved yourself dealing with an angry woman if you'd have told her the truth. I don't think she'd want Winslow in the building if she knew what kind of man he is." Hal looked again toward the doorway Marisa had gone through and took a deep breath. "We're burning golden time, Lee. We need to get back to work. I came to apologize for Maddie's mistake. I've been preaching for my people to follow the plans. Once in a while they blow it. Guess maybe I'm working them too hard."

Lee stroked his jaw thoughtfully and stared at the empty doorway leading to the hall. Then he jerked to his full height, stiffened his spine and focused on his foreman. "We're all working too hard, Bristo, but that doesn't mean we shouldn't get back at it."

Chapter Twelve

Marisa went through the following weeks on automatic pilot. Between her classes, renovating her apartment, her job at the restaurant and taking care of her mother, she barely had time to sleep.

She avoided contact with Lee, but she couldn't keep him out of her thoughts. She loved him. She had no doubt about that. But she couldn't have him. Her only choice as to how to handle Lee was to forget him. That would not be easy. She'd never be able to chase away memories of being held and kissed by the man she loved.

She didn't want to forget their romantic dinner at *El Cielo de los Estrellas,* their evening in the gazebo or any other moment they'd spent together in warmth, friendship and love. What she really had to concentrate on was dismissing any future with Lee. That she could do. Couldn't she?

The renovations on the apartments had progressed nicely. All the tenants were meeting their deadlines. Marisa noted that Lee had put in plenty of overtime helping some of the neighbors so they wouldn't be late. But she concluded that his reason for the extra work was to keep his project on time, not to be neighborly. Time was money, and money was Lee's reason for all his actions.

That wasn't exactly true. Lee did have his moments of kindness. She had to admit that.

Marisa was proud of the improvements she saw when she walked through her building. The modern apartments tucked inside the beauty of one of Houston's lovely, old brick structures took on the homey appearance Lee had said he wanted to achieve. Sarafina had completed a couple of her wall hangings. They greeted people as they entered through the new security system on the ground floor.

The tenants of the building couldn't have been more pleased with the improvements, with Lee or with themselves and their contributions to the new look of their building.

Marisa went to apartment 2-E and 2-F, the three-bedroom unit the Cortezes were going to buy, to help with the renovations. In exchange for her work, Ruben and his son were going to do all the painting in Marisa's apartment.

Tia Conlin, the hairdresser who lived in 4-C, was also working for Ruben under the same agreement as Marisa. She'd barely seen the beautician in the last two weeks. After having worked with Tia in Randi's and Jorge's apartments, Marisa missed the light-hearted chatter and tidbits of gossip Tia provided. Work was always more fun with Tia. Marisa was happy that they would be working together again.

"I see you were quite successful with your matchmaking work with Monte and Molly," Marisa said as she applied finish remover to ancient oak molding she and Tia were restoring. The beautician was a perpetual match-maker. She'd coupled Monte Vargas, one of Lee's plumbers, with Molly Winn in 4-E. The last time Marisa worked with Tia, the hairdresser had said she was going to find someone for Lee. She'd suggested fixing him up with Maddie, the carpenter who Lee had been scolding the last time Marisa talked with him. The thought of Lee being with anyone else didn't sit well with Marisa, but there wasn't a thing she could do about it.

Tia waved a casual hand. "That was easy. Those two were born for each other. Monte even cut off that ponytail he's had for the last fifteen years. Molly mentioned once that she didn't care for long hair on men, and he found scissors, cut it off and gave it to her."

Marisa chuckled and tugged at her rubber gloves. "What did she do with it?"

"She tossed it in the trash, yanked him into a corner, made sure no one was looking and planted a big kiss on his eager little lips."

"Did she tell you that?"

Tia's grin lit her face. She shook her head. "She didn't have to. I saw the whole thing myself. I was looking."

"Love in the middle of plaster dust and paint fumes. How romantic." Marisa tried to sound sarcastic, but hadn't she fallen for Lee in similar circumstances?

Tia tried to scratch her dark skinned cheek with her wrist, avoiding the use of her gloved hand which was full of stain remover. "I struck out with Maddie and Lee." She scratched her cheek again. "I could be wrong, but I get the very distinct impression that Lee is already in love with someone else."

"Would you hand me that rag, Tia?" A change of subject wouldn't hurt, Marisa decided.

Tia handed Marisa the rag. "What about you, Marisa? You think Lee might have his eye on someone here or anyone else for that matter?"

"I need the can of stain remover too," Marisa said.

"I've noticed you haven't been very friendly with Lee, especially the last few weeks. Have you got something against him?"

Marisa took a deep breath and blew it out. Tia wasn't going to allow the subject to move off of Lee Ramon. "As a matter of fact, I do," she replied in a huff.

"You do, huh? Like what?"

Marisa raised her hand and waved it around the room. "Look at where we are, Tia. Whose apartment are we renovating now?"

"Ruben and Olivia's."

"No, I mean who did this apartment belong to before?"

"Well, the efficiency unit was Roger Winslow's, and the two-bedroom apartment was vacant for quite a while. I think it was the Flavios who lived there last."

"But the Flavios have been gone a long time. Roger left recently. Lee threw him out because he was a week late with his rent. That's a pretty rotten thing to do to a man like Roger who has so many problems. That's what I've got against L.C. Ramon." She nodded toward Tia. "You know about Roger's stint in Vietnam, his drinking and trouble with holding jobs. I'll never understand a complete lack of compassion like Lee showed toward Roger, a veteran who deserves our gratitude."

"You're right about Roger's problems, Marisa, but Lee didn't evict him just for being a week late with his rent. Lee would never do a thing like that."

"Would do it. Did do it," Marisa said firmly.

Tia put a hand on her hip and shook her head defiantly.

"No way, Marisa. You are one hundred percent totally dead wrong. Lee did not evict Roger for being late with his rent."

Marisa's heart stopped for what felt like minutes. Her face froze in a stare toward Tia. "He didn't?" Marisa wet her lips. Could Tia be right? She did always know everything going on with the people in the building. She decided she needed to hear Tia's explanation. "Then why did Lee evict Roger?"

"Roger was fencing stolen goods. Lee went to see Roger because he'd heard Roger lost his latest job. He was going to offer him work. When Roger let him into his apartment, Lee saw a dozen DVD players, a bunch of televisions, stereos and who knows what else?" Tia rubbed her nose with her wrist. "Lee didn't have any choice. He promised us a safe building. Thieves have to go."

"Roger was a thief? I can't believe it. How do you know all this?"

"I overheard Lee talking with his foreman."

Marisa was stunned. Was Tia's information true?

"This wasn't the first time Roger had been involved in crime, Marisa," Tia said, widening her dark eyes.

"Although he'd cleaned up his act lately, for some reason he went back to old ways."

Marisa stared past Tia a long moment, then glanced at her again. "How sad."

"Sad for Roger that he got back into his criminal ways, but think how frightening it has been for his victims." Tia shook her head and bit her lip. "Lee did the only thing he could do to protect us."

And she'd accused him of being heartless. Marisa ripped the rubber gloves from her hands. She threw them and her rag to the floor. "I've got to go."

"Hey," Tia protested, "you can't leave me with all this work."

Marisa turned back to Tia. "I won't be gone long. I'll work twice as hard when I get back."

As she searched the building for Lee, Marisa questioned whether or not Tia had all the facts straight. If she did, then Marisa was as wrong as she could be about Lee. An apology wouldn't be enough to make up for the terrible things she'd said to him.

Yet they *were* currently doing renovations in Roger's apartment. Roger had said Lee wanted him out so the remodeling could begin to convert his unit and the two-bedroom apartment next door into another three-bedroom as soon as possible. What Roger said made sense. It too could be the truth.

Marisa located Lee on the fifth floor in his apartment. His door was ajar. She pushed it a little farther open, and Lee turned toward her.

"Marisa, come in, please." He walked toward her.

Heat began to fill her cheeks. Eating crow had never been easy for her, but what she'd been wrong about this time, if indeed she was wrong, caused Lee a great deal of pain—especially if he cared for her as deeply as she believed he did. Straight off, she was giving him the benefit of the doubt by trusting in Tia's words. She owed him that.

Marisa bit her lip and looked up at him. "I'm sorry, Lee."

He tucked his blue work shirt into his jeans. "About what?"

"That I jumped to the wrong conclusion about Roger."

"What makes you think you were wrong?"

"You mean I wasn't?"

"I didn't say that."

She reached out and gripped Lee's arm. "I know what happened." She bit her lip again. "At least I think I know."

He covered the hand on his arm with his. "And now you're sorry for what?"

"For calling you heartless." She shook her head. "You're not. I'm the one who was wrong. I know now that Roger was involved in criminal activity, that you had no choice but to evict him immediately." She let go of his arm and pulled her hand back. "That is true, isn't it, Lee?"

"I hate talking about other people's business, Marisa, but," he said, closing his eyes before he looked at her again, "I'm afraid what you heard is correct. Roger was involved in criminal activity." He reached toward her and stroked a single finger along her jaw. "I wished you'd have trusted me, Marisa."

She closed her eyes at the touch of his gentle fingers. "Me too," she whispered.

"Marisa," Lee said softly, "open your eyes."

She looked up at him as he stroked her cheek one more time.

He pulled his hand back. "I don't like ill will between us. I hope we can get back on the right track."

A lump formed in her throat. "And what track is that?" she asked, needing to hear from his own lips that he forgave her and wanted to have her back in his life.

He stepped toward her and cupped her face with his hands. "I think you know where we were headed. I'd like to continue in that same direction."

"Then you forgive me?" she said, placing her hands over his forearms as he continued to hold her cheeks.

"Of course." He bent toward her and kissed her lightly. "I should have come to you and explained things a long

time ago. I never should have let this rancor go on between us. That wasn't the right way to treat someone I
care about as much as I care about you, Marisa." He gave
her another feather-light kiss and stepped back. "Are you
working in Ruben's apartment today?"

"Yes."

"Good. I'll stop by later. We'll talk and make plans to
go somewhere together, maybe *El Cielo* again. We had
such a nice time there, and I need to talk to you about
something very important."

Lee was making things so easy for her. If he had treated
her as unfairly as she treated him, she didn't think she
would have let him off the hook as easily. "*El Cielo* would
be wonderful, Lee."

"Great," he said, smiling at her and stroking her cheek
with his fingers. "I'll come by in an hour or so and set up
a day and time to go."

Marisa returned his smile. "I'll see you then." She
turned and left Lee's apartment a whole lot happier than
she was when she had arrived. Life was wonderful.

Lee tried to get to Ruben's apartment at the time he
promised Marisa he would be there, but he didn't make it.
Shortly after she had left his flat, a messenger arrived. It
looked as though Hal was exacting his revenge on Lee for
allowing the sweat equity program to take place. A judge
would soon be handing down a ruling on Hal's complaint
that Lee violated the agreement to use only union workers
on the renovation project. Lee's attorney said things did
not look good.

The phone calls he had to make to do whatever he could
to avoid a ruling that would surely cost him the last of his

fortune couldn't wait. By the time Lee had finished his calls, he was almost an hour late in meeting Marisa.

When he finally arrived at Ruben's apartment, Marisa was no where in sight. He asked Ruben and Olivia where his lady went, but neither of them knew.

As he went back into the hall, Randi found him. "Lee, I've been looking for you. Marisa called me. Her mother has taken a turn for the worse. They had to take her to a special clinic right away. Marisa wanted me to find you and tell you what happened. She says she may be away for a few days, Lee. She told me I should tell you she was sorry, but I don't know what for."

"Never mind that. Was she alright? I mean did she sound like she was handling things well enough?" He wanted to go to her immediately.

"She's been a rock when it comes to caring for her mother, Lee. She'll be fine. She's always fine."

He nodded and stroked his fingers along the line of his jaw. "I'm sure she'll get along alright." He should be with her, but he couldn't leave now. Everything he owned was at risk. "Where were they taking her mother? Did she tell you?"

Randi shook her head as a look of panic crossed her face. "I don't know! I'm sorry, all she said was that they were taking her to a special clinic. She sounded so calm, I began to panic for her and I didn't think. I should have asked more questions."

"And I should be with her. No one deserves to go through what she's going through all alone." He made up his mind. Dollars be damned, Marisa needed him. He wasn't going to let her down.

"But, Lee, she's already left. She was on her way out

the door when she called me a half hour ago. I'm sorry I didn't get to you sooner. I did the best I could."

He took hold of Randi's shoulders and tried to calm her. "It's alright, Randi. Don't worry about it, I'll find her."

She shook her head. "You can't. You aren't family. The privacy laws won't let her nursing home tell you where Ariane was taken. She might not even be in the state anymore. We have no way of knowing."

"I'll find a way." Nothing would stop him, not when Marisa needed him.

"Lee," Randi said, reaching out for him, "she's alright. She'll be alright. Both of them will be alright. We've got to believe that."

He nodded toward her. "I've got to go." He headed back to his apartment. He located the master keys for the apartments and went to Marisa's unit and let himself in.

Things were in disarray from the remodeling that was going, but he found her desk and began to look through it for any kind of clue that might tell him where Marisa's mother may have been taken. Perhaps she'd been at a clinic before, and she was taken to the same one again.

Lee felt like an intruder as he rifled through Marisa's things. He hated invading her privacy, but he hated more that he couldn't be with her when she needed him. And he couldn't get to her unless he could figure out where she went.

Lee quickly realized his search was fruitless. He found nothing that would give him any insight as to where Mrs. Orlando may have been taken.

He plopped down in the chair near the desk, accidentally knocking a loose paper from the top of the desk onto the floor. He picked it up and looked at it. Marisa's contract for her sweat equity reminded him that her completion date would arrive in three days. If the work on her apartment was not finished by then, Marisa would lose her apartment. Lee couldn't stop it or change the contract either. He was bound to follow the letter of the contract. He was bound by his agreements with his partners.

He looked around the flat and estimated the amount of work that remained to meet the completion standards. There was no way he could do Marisa's work all by himself, not with all the other demands on his time.

He dropped his head into his hands. He couldn't be with her to lend her support as she went through this trying ordeal with her mother. He couldn't get her renovation finished for her by the time her completion date rolled around. Some friend he was turning out to be. He'd intended to ask Marisa on their next evening together to share his life. He had intended to promise he would devote himself to making her happy. He'd planned to propose marriage to her because he knew he couldn't live without her.

What kind of husband would he be when he was so useless to her now?

He rubbed his hands over his face and sat in the chair a moment longer. Then he got up and straightened the mess he'd made as he looked through Marisa's desk.

A knock sounded at the door.

Lee went to the door and opened it. He looked down to find Ruben Cortez.

"My boy will be along in a minute with the paint and brushes. I've got the drop cloths. Is Marisa here? Did you find her?"

Lee furrowed his brows. "She's not here, Ruben. Are you supposed to paint for her?"

"Yeah. She helped me today in my apartment. She helped me many times already. I am to prime the walls if they are sanded. If they need more sanding, I could do that too."

Lee looked around the apartment, then back at Ruben. "Marisa had to go out of town, but I don't think she'd mind you working while she is gone. Come on in." He opened the door wide. Once Ruben was inside, Lee knew what he could do to help Marisa. He wasted no time jumping into action.

Marisa's summer had been a rough one, but it hadn't been as difficult as the last four days. She was glad to be back from Dallas.

As the cab let her off at her apartment building, she stood outside and looked up at the third floor stairway window.

She was happy that the clinic in Dallas had been able to help. Her mother was back at the nursing home, and the doctors said her setback would eventually turn out to be a blessing in disguise. They were able to help her mother improve the little movement she had in her arms. They were hopeful that she would eventually be able to talk and move a great deal more too.

That was very good news.

Marisa blinked back tears. Along with the good came the bad, she remembered as she continued to stare at the window on the third floor. In a week or two she'd be homeless. For the second time in her life, she wouldn't have a place to live.

Tears slid down her cheeks. She didn't know if she could stand displacement again. But she'd have to stand it.

There was no getting around it, she'd missed her deadline. She lacked the down payment she needed to buy her home. She'd have to find another place to live.

Marisa took a deep breath and began to put one foot in front of the other. She went inside and took the elevator to the third floor. She shuffled down the hall to her apartment and put the key inside the lock.

When she opened the door, she was greeted with the shouts of nearly a dozen people.

"She's here!" Ruben yelled.

"It's Marisa!" Cliff hollered.

"Surprise!" Her neighbors screamed.

Marisa's shock would have been evident to a dead man. "What's going on?"

Lee walked up to her and put his arms around her. "How's your mother?"

"She's better."

He let her go and smiled down at her. "We all pitched in and finished the remodeling, Marisa. We've met your completion date. You're a home owner again, sunshine."

Tears welled in her eyes. She shook her head vigorously. "No!" She looked at every person in the room and shook her head again. "No," she whispered.

If she'd been sad about losing her apartment before, she was stricken with intense grief over her predicament now. She turned and bolted down the hall toward the elevator. "No," she said as she pushed the down button, begging the elevator to come and take her away.

Lee came up behind her as the elevator doors opened. "Marisa, wait. What's wrong? Your renovation is finished. The apartment is yours. All that's left is to make the rest of the down payment from the money you earned at Pat

O'Reiley's this summer, sign the deed and you will own your home again just like you wanted, just like the others in the building have done."

Tears streamed down her cheeks. She stepped into the elevator and held the door open as she spoke. "No, Lee. I've lost everything. I don't have the money I earned at the restaurant. I had to give it to the clinic for Mom's treatment. I have only a few dollars to my name. I could barely pay the cab driver who brought me home." She let go of the door, and it started to close. "Thank everyone for finishing my apartment, Lee."

The doors closed and Marisa completed her descent. She'd give her neighbors an hour or two to clear out of her apartment. Then she'd go home and start packing. Tomorrow she'd start looking for a new place to live.

Chapter Thirteen

Lee couldn't believe what he'd heard. After all Marisa had done to be able to buy her apartment, after the way she worked to help her neighbors stay on and keep her community in tact . . . he muttered a series of curses.

It wasn't fair. No one deserved a home of her own more than Marisa.

Sarafina walked up to Lee and stood next to him. "It looks like we won't be needing that coffee cake I brought for Marisa's celebration," she said, laying her hand on his shoulder. "The guest of honor has disappeared."

Lee looked at her and forced himself to calm down. "She'll be back," he said, half wondering if she would.

"Of course she will." Sarafina drew her hand back and pushed the up button to summon the elevator. "She's got everything she wanted now, a home of her own, the friendship of her neighbors and her community closer than ever. I think the joy was too much for her. I've seen people run from happiness before. They always come back."

165

Lee didn't have the heart to tell Sarafina what really happened. Like everyone else, she'd find out in time. "I suppose you're right."

"I usually am," she said, grinning. "A person doesn't get to be as old as I am without learning a few things in life."

Lee smiled back at her.

She patted him on the shoulder as the elevator doors began to open. "She'll be back," she assured him. "But if she isn't," she added as she stepped on the elevator, "you go get her. Don't let her get away, Lee."

The elevator doors closed.

As he thought about Sarafina's last statement, Lee wondered if his feelings for Marisa were obvious to everyone but the object of his affections. He had to tell her that he loved her. As soon as Marisa returned, he had to make her understand how strongly he felt about her.

Marisa ended up at the library, then a diner that served fifty-cent coffee, then walking along the streets in her neighborhood. She didn't want to go home. She shuddered at the irony of her feelings. On these last few days while she still had a home, she didn't want to return there.

Had it been only four or five days since she'd decided life was wonderful? Had it been only that long since she'd made peace with Lee and they'd begun to make plans for the future? Things changed so much over the past few days.

First, there was the awful phone call about her mother's sudden setback. It came as she enjoyed one of the happiest moments of her life, dreaming about being with Lee again. Second, when Marisa reached the hospital where her mother had been taken, she learned her mom would have to go to the clinic where she'd been after she'd suffered her first stroke. While at the clinic, the days began to tick off one by one, and Marisa realized she'd never be able to meet the completion date for her sweat equity contract. So when the clinic asked for a payment on services rendered for her mother, Marisa knew she had nothing to lose by turning over nearly all the money she had. She'd be in breach of contract and lose all her sweat equity anyway. She might as well make as big a payment as she could toward her mother's expenses and save money on interest charges.

When she arrived home and saw that her neighbors had saved her from breaking her contracted agreement with Lee, it was as though she'd been punched in the face with the irony of it all. She could have made other arrangements for payment with the clinic. She could have given them only the amount of the money above what she needed to complete the down payment on her condo and agreed to pay the rest in installments. If she'd done that, she'd still have her home, her neighbors, the community she loved so much.

Now she had nothing.

Marisa returned home after midnight. She left before six the next morning.

Over the next few days she barely spent any time at home. She went to her classes, studied and played catch up for the time she lost in school while she was away, and spent as much time with her mother as she could. She didn't need to be away from home as much as she was, she just couldn't stand to be in the lovely apartment she was about to lose. It hurt too much to be so acutely aware of what she was not going to have anymore.

And she didn't want to run into Lee. As much as she needed his arms around her, comforting her, caring for her, she couldn't face losing him anymore than she could face losing her home. And she would lose him now. He'd done so much for her to help her keep her home, and now she would lose it. She'd let him down. She was so ashamed. She'd spent so much time being nasty to him, and he'd quickly forgiven her. But how many of her mistakes should Lee have to overlook?

Marisa shivered and shook her head. She didn't deserve a man like Lee.

Several days after she returned to Houston, Marisa met Tia at the nursing home. "What are you doing here?" she asked, surprised to find the beautician walking the familiar halls.

"I brought Harry and Cecelia over. They've got a friend who was admitted a couple of days ago, and they wanted to visit her. I offered them a ride because I figured I might find you here. Don't you know all of us are worried sick about you? We've been searching for you everywhere."

"But why? I'm okay."

"I can see you're getting around alright, but you don't look okay at all," Tia said, eyeing Marisa carefully. "Your hair's a disaster, your clothes are wrinkled and you look like you haven't slept more than five hours a night for a week. Worse yet, you've got wrinkles creeping out along the skin around your eyes."

"Sounds like I'd better check into this place before I keel over," Marisa said sardonically.

Tia's smile lit her beautiful face. Marisa had always admired her friend's flawless ebony skin, the perfect shape of her brows and her sparkling dark eyes. "You see? Who am I going to tease if you're not around? And who is going to tease me back? You've got to come home once in a while, Marisa." She stepped closer and lowered her voice. "Besides, I need you to listen to all my juicy tidbits. It's no fun knowing the scoop on everything without being able to share it with friends." She stepped back. "So you want to ride home with Harry, Cecelia and me?"

Marisa shrugged. It seemed that Tia didn't have the scoop on everything as she thought. She obviously didn't yet know that Marisa would soon have no home to go to, unless her luck improved in the next few days and she found another apartment. She hadn't been able to find a new place so far, not that she'd had time to look very hard. "Maybe I'll catch a ride with you."

"I wish you would," she said. "We all miss you." Tia bit her cheek and looked at Marisa tentatively. "I've got some news that I'm rather upset about. I'd like to share it with someone. I know you've got enough problems of your own with you mom's health and all, but, if you don't mind, could we talk?"

Marisa decided it might be a good idea to focus on someone else's troubles for a while and stop worrying about her own. "Let's go over there," she said, pointing to an alcove holding lush plants and soft chairs. "It'll be private, and the chairs are very inviting."

The ladies walked together to the alcove and made themselves comfortable.

"What's wrong, Tia? You didn't have trouble fulfilling your contract or anything, did you?" Marisa asked when Tia seemed hesitant to begin.

She waved a hand casually. "No, nothing like that. I had plenty of help coming in on time." A sly grin crept over her face. "From Ben Hargrove."

"Lee's carpenter?"

Tia nodded and showed more of her beautiful teeth. "He's a dream, isn't he?" She reached to touch Marisa's hand. "Funny thing about Ben and me is someone turned the tables on me. Sarafina caught us both out in the hall one day, me taking renovation materials into my apartment, Ben coming out of one of the other apartments, and she asked the two of us to help her with something. I don't remember what it was. Next thing I know, she's setting us up with a dinner date at a restaurant one of her former student's owns." Tia chuckled and pulled her hand back. "Can you imagine that? The matchmaker being matched with the perfect guy? I have to give Sarafina credit as well as my thanks. It's only been a couple of weeks, but I'm head over heels for Ben."

"That's wonderful," Marisa said, laying her hand over her heart. "I thought from the way you talked you had a problem you wanted to talk about, but this is great between you and Ben. He's a very nice young man, not to mention gorgeous."

"He's finer than ten pounds of chocolate candy and a hundred times as sweet. But my new-found relationship with Ben isn't all I have to talk to you about, Marisa." The dreamy look in her dark eyes dissipated. "Ben told me something rather shocking. I thought you should know about it. I figured you'd find out about it eventually, but I wanted to ease you into it if I could, especially since you were instrumental in making the sweat equity program work." She gripped Marisa's hand. "Now don't go holding yourself responsible, honey. It wasn't your fault. Lee made his own decisions."

What on earth could she be talking about? "My fault?" Marisa shook her head and pulled her hand away from Tia. "I have no idea what you mean. Did something go wrong with someone's contract? Did someone lose their equity?"

Tia shook her head. "We tenants are just fine. Those of us who aren't finished with our contracts are running on time. None of us will let any of the tenants breach their contracts." She lifted her chin. "We took care of your condo, didn't we?"

Marisa forced a smile and tried to show gratitude, despite the fact that her friends' efforts were all for naught. "I appreciate everything all of you did for me."

"We take care of our own. That's the way our building community has been. But our gains have turned into losses for someone we've all grown very fond of, Marisa."

She wrinkled her forehead. "Losses? For whom?"

"Lee."

"What?"

"Ben told me what happened." Tia shifted uncomfortably in her chair. "You know Hal Bristo, the foreman for the renovation project?"

"Sure."

"Ben told me Hal is a union man all the way. He made Lee promise that only union people would work on the renovation. It was in their contracted agreement. When the sweat equity program first came up, Hal tried to put a stop to it. Ben, he didn't care. He thought the equity program was good. He liked helping the tenants keep their homes. But Hal didn't like us doing our own work because we didn't belong to any construction union. Lee

told him since we were working on our own homes, we
didn't come under the agreement Lee had made with Hal
and the other owners that only union people would work
on the renovation."

"That makes sense. Home owners shouldn't have to belong to a union to work on their own homes. It sounds like
this Hal just wanted to cause trouble."

"Well," Tia said, placing a hand on Marisa's arm and
drawing it back, "whatever his reasons, he took the matter
to court, and he won his argument. He got a huge settlement against Lee."

"No!" Marisa said, bolting to her feet. She walked to
the window and leaned forward, bracing herself on the
sill. "Our sweat equity program cost Lee?" She spun
around and looked at Tia. "He lost money because he
gave us a chance to own our homes?"

"He lost lots of money, according to Ben," Tia said,
walking over to her. She folded her arms. "Stinks, doesn't
it?"

"To say the least." Marisa wanted to go straight to Lee
and apologize to him for pushing him so hard to get involved with all the tenants in the program that cost him so
dearly. "Ben told you all of this? Do the other tenants
know?" If Tia knew, most likely everyone knew.

She shook her head. "I understand it's hard to believe
with my tendency to tell all I know, but you're the only
one I've told, Marisa. I figured you should know because
you were instrumental in getting the sweat equity program off the ground."

Marisa's gut tied itself into a knot. "If you're trying to
make me feel guilty, it's working."

"No, honey, I'm not trying to make you feel anything. I
just wanted you to know what Ben told me. How you feel

about the knowledge or what you do with it is up to you. I just thought you should know, that's all."

Marisa turned and glanced into the mirror that hung over one of the chairs. She ran her fingers through her hair. "I'm a mess," she whispered. "Life's a mess." She plopped down in a chair. "Everything's a mess, Tia."

Tia sat next to Marisa. "There isn't a thing in the world I can do about life's problems, honey, but I can do something with that hair of yours. And, if your mom has her feminine fix-ups here, I can put a little color in your cheeks, too. Want to have a mini makeover while we wait for Harry and Cecelia?"

Marisa forced a smile. "Why not?" She knew she'd have to find Lee as soon as she got back to the condos. She should make herself look presentable.

Tia and Marisa went to Ariane's room. The beautician fixed Marisa's hair and makeup first, then she made Marisa's mother look prettier than her daughter had seen her in a long time. Her mother seemed pleased with what Tia had done, according to the sparkle that came into her eyes when she looked into the mirror Tia held up for her.

Once the mini makeovers were complete, Tia and Marisa met Harry and Cecelia in the waiting area. The four of them returned to the condos. As her friends went inside, Marisa excused herself. She needed to go to the convenience store up the street to get some things before she went want to find Lee.

A few minutes later, she returned to her building with a bag containing what she wanted. She went inside and pressed the up button on the elevator. When she entered the car, she hit number five. She was going straight to Lee's apartment. She had to see him immediately.

The lift stopped at the second floor, and Marisa let go

of a muttered word of disgust. She was in no mood to talk to anyone or be delayed in any manner. All she wanted was to see Lee as soon as possible.

When the doors of the elevator opened, Lee stepped inside.

Chapter Fourteen

"Marisa, I've been looking for you for days." Lee stepped next to her and touched her chin. "Where have you been?"

He looked good. He looked so down right heavenly good. She stepped toward him and wrapped her arms around him. "I'm happy to see you, Lee." She set the bag she was carrying on the floor.

He held her close and kissed the top of her head. "Me too, sunshine. I've been worried about you."

She pulled back and gave him a stunned look. "You've been worried about me? With all that has happened with you, you're worried about me?" She hugged him hard. "Oh, Lee, if I could take it all back I would. I never meant to hurt you." She squeezed him as hard as she could.

"Marisa," he said, gently loosening her grip on him. He turned toward the panel in the lift and hit the stop button. "What are you talking about? We're not moving another inch until you tell me what's going on."

175

She stared at the numbered panel Lee stood next to. "You stalled the elevator."

"I know."

"But why? We could talk in your apartment. We don't have to talk here."

"I don't want any distractions. I've been searching for you for days. Now that I have found you, nothing is going to interrupt us." He stepped toward her and brushed her hair back from her face. "Now, before I tell you what I've been trying to tell you since the last time I saw you, I want you to explain what you're sorry for. I have no idea what you're talking about. Unless . . . ," he stepped back and folded his arms. "Have you been avoiding me? Is that why I haven't been able to find you? Is that what you're sorry for?"

She shook her head and leaned against the wall, gripping the handrail to steady herself. "I wish what I had done to you had been that simple." She shook her head once more. "No, Lee, I've done far worse than that. I learned what has happened to you just a little while ago. You lost a legal battle because you made it possible for the tenants of this building to buy their homes."

"Who told you that?"

"I'd rather not say. It doesn't matter, unless it's a lie."

He dropped his arms to his sides and tilted his head to one side. "It isn't a lie. I thought I was on solid ground when I offered the sweat equity program, but a judge saw it differently." He shrugged casually. "Easy come, easy go."

"You say that as though you don't care that your money is gone. Aren't you upset?"

"Sure I'm upset. I should have hired a better lawyer," he said, giving her a disdainful grin. "Fact is, I lost a bundle on my last job due to a complicated set of circum-

stances. My losses were so great that I had to take on partners to do this renovation. I've never done that before.
This settlement against me will take a good deal of the remainder of my capital."

"Lee . . ." Her knees went weak and her head started to
swim. She gripped the railing tightly. "It's worse than I
ever imagined," she said weakly. "You've really lost all
your money?" She'd never been as wealthy as Lee, but
she knew what it was like to lose everything she'd worked
so hard to earn.

He went to her and took her into his arms. "It's only
money, Marisa. I can earn more. I wasn't born rich. I was
poor as a cat when I was a kid. I started working in construction when I was fourteen. I knew this was the kind of
work I wanted to do for the rest of my life. I started with a
thousand dollars, a strong back and a ton of hope when I
was twenty-one years old. I'd put myself through college,
and I was ready to set the world on fire. I did just that, too.
By the time I reached thirty, I had earned a good deal
more money than I had ever dreamed I would earn in a
lifetime."

"And now it's gone, Lee?"

"Well, not all of it. I've got enough to start over with a
small building or two, maybe some duplexes or four-
plexes in the right neighborhoods. And I've got enough to
buy a home. I sold mine when I bought this building."

"I was wondering why you lived here in an efficiency
apartment instead of in a house somewhere."

"It was convenient for me while I worked. I couldn't
live in my other buildings because they weren't livable
when I bought them. I had always bought abandoned
buildings before." He waved his hand through the air.
"We're getting off track."

"What track? The one where I talked you into offering the sweat equity program, and you ended up losing all your money?"

He took her hands. "Don't blame yourself. I made my own choices, and I wouldn't change them for anything. Besides, I didn't have that much left to lose. And, as I told you, I'll earn it back. In fact, I'm excited to be able to meet the challenge again." He grinned at her. "You know, Marisa, being rich isn't as exciting as working to become rich."

She shrugged and pulled her hands away from him. "I wouldn't know about that."

"Would you like to?"

"Would I like to what?"

"Know what it feels like to become wealthy?"

She chuckled at the outrageous suggestion he made. "Who wouldn't?"

"Then experience it with me, Marisa. Let me share with you as you've shared with me."

"Are you serious?"

He moved closer to her. "I'm very serious," he said in a low husky voice. "You showed me a wealth I never knew existed, Marisa, something much more valuable than money. You introduced me to people who have become true friends. You've taught me what it means to be part of a community." He took her into his arms. "And you taught me how to love." He stroked her hair gently. "I love you, Marisa, and I want you to be my wife."

If Lee hadn't been holding her tightly when she heard the words she'd longed for him to say, she'd have fallen down. "You love me?"

"Very much."

She sent him a naughty grin. "Show me," she said coyly.

He knew exactly what she meant because he wasted no time in touching his lips to hers for a long, slow, breath-stealing, heart-stopping, toe-curling kiss.

When he pulled back, Marisa said what was in her heart, what she'd wanted to tell Lee ever since they'd been together in the gazebo. "I love you, Lee Ramon. I'm going to love you for the rest of my life."

"You're sure?" he asked, grinning at her.

"Absolutely," she said, filling her face with the smile that began deep inside her.

"You'll marry me then? And share in my business with me?"

"I'll marry you, yes. I'll share in your business as much as I can, but I don't want to give up my teaching."

"Share with me as little or as much as you want with business, Marisa, but share everything else in my life completely."

"I'm so happy, Lee. I'm happier than I ever thought I could be."

"Good, because I'm not finished yet asking you for favors."

She gave him another coy grin. "I hope you'll always ask me for favors, Lee Ramon."

He chuckled and held her close. Then he kissed her as thoroughly as he had a minute before. He kissed her again. "I will, sunshine. You just wait and see." He kissed her lightly and let her go. "But that is not what I meant."

"It isn't?"

"No," he said, lifting a lock of hair over her shoulder. "What I meant was that I hope you will like the home I've chosen for us to live in. I hope you don't mind that I was bold enough to choose a home without first consulting you. Would you grant me that favor?"

Marisa scowled and grinned at him at the same time. "What have you done?" she asked suspiciously. "And how did you get to be so sure of yourself?"

"As for being sure of myself . . . I don't know if I fit that description, but I did make up my mind that I'd pester you to marry me until you said yes. I didn't know how long that might take." He took her in her arms and kissed her again. "But I'm sure glad I didn't have to wait long for you to agree to be my wife." He let go of her and stepped back. "My wife. I love the sound of that."

Marisa felt a thrill course through her body. "Me too," she said. "Now where is our new home to be?"

"Our home," he said on a sigh. "I like the sound of that, too." He focused on her a long moment, then he said, "It isn't anything palatial, Marisa. In fact, it's rather humble, but it will be ours, and that's all that matters."

She folded her arms and sent him an impatient grin. "Will you just tell me already where we are going to live?"

He made her wait a moment longer before he answered. Then he said, "How about 3-C right here in this building, across the hall from Randi and Cliff Jarvis and next to Ana and Jorge Garcia?"

"My apartment?"

"Our apartment," he said, taking her into his arms. "I put through the original deal you agreed to. I paid the balance of down payment on top of what you earned in sweat equity. The condo is in your name, Marisa." He held her closer. "But you will let me live there after we're married, won't you?" he asked, teasing her.

"You'd better," she said. She stretched up and kissed him the way she planned to kiss him the rest of her life.

When they released their grasp on each other, Lee

smiled down at her and took her hand. "Let's go home," he said softly.

She reached up and kissed his cheek. As she stepped forward, she nudged the bag she'd set on the floor.

"What's in here?" Lee asked as he reached for the bag.

Marisa took the plastic sack from him and held it shut. "Something you won't need anymore, a bachelor's snack, root beer and donuts, like we shared on the day we met. I was bringing them up to your apartment to have while I tried to convince you to forgive me for pushing you into the sweat equity program."

He took the sack from her. "We can't let fine food like this go to waste. We'll go home and celebrate an end to our single lives and a beginning to our married life, full of home-cooked food from now on."

Marisa pushed the button on the panel that put the elevator back in motion toward the third floor. "I like the sound of that," she said, cuddling against Lee. "And I'm glad you're going to start taking cooking lessons so we can enjoy some of that home cooking you promised."

The elevator doors opened.

"What?" Lee asked incredulous. "Me cook? No way. That's going to be your job."

Marisa went ahead of him to condo 3-C shaking her head. "Don't be silly. I can't boil water."

Lee caught up with her and took her into his arms. "If neither one of us can cook, I guess we'll have to reserve a permanent table at Pat O'Reiley's."

"I guess so."

Lee kissed Marisa's cheek. "Let's go inside, I'm famished."

"We'll have peanut butter sandwiches with our donuts and root beer," Marisa said as she opened the door.

He stopped her before she went inside and took hold of her chin with his fingers. "It isn't food that I want, Marisa. It's being with you. I've waited an eternity to be with you, sunshine. I'm starved for the sight of you." He kissed her sweetly. "You're all I need, everything I've ever wanted."

Marisa took his hand. "Let's go inside, Lee. We're home."

F
SHA

Ever so Humble
$20.00
2/16/05